Perfect

a love story

J. C. Soucier

Outskirts Press, Inc.
Denver, Colorado

*I never started out with the intention of writing
a book ~
It was really to be a Christmas gift to my family.*

*However, because of their encouragement, enthusiasm and belief
in me, I embarked on an adventure that took me beyond my wildest
dreams.*

*Dear Dr. and Mrs. Soucier I give to you and to the world this en-
chanting true story of my perfect gift.*

~ Forever my love ~

Cover Design – Stephanie Soucier

ACKNOWLEDGEMENTS

"Teamwork divides the task and multiplies the success. ~ Author Unknown.

Although this is my true story, friends and family made it all happen for me. I was blessed with the best team in the world. Thank you to my family who was and continues to be my inspiration. They encouraged me to tell this story to the world. They were my sensitive critics and personal cheerleaders whose never ending enthusiasm, motivation and faith gave me the energy and spirit that I needed to pursue publishing my manuscript.

To my dear friend, Nancy Snow, who from the very beginning and to this day, has walked beside me step for step as together we ventured into this unknown territory.

Thank you to Ric Dreyser for doing a colossal amount of research and building the springboard that catapulted me into this whole new world. Thanks to my long time confidante, Pati Keene who read and re-read my work multiple times 'til her eyes crossed and words slurred.

To Barbara Hough who pulled out all stops and offered me opportunities beyond imagination. Lisa McPhee for her expedient and most efficient proofreading, editing, guidance and flair that added those finishing touches. To Debbie Blackwood for giving me wings and along with Cathy Goodwin for being the first responders 35 years ago. To my newly found sister Joy Jones, Georgine Ouellette, Yvette Rousseau, Dick Snow, Janet Spellman, Bob Spencer, Mitchell Clyde Thomas and J. Peter Thompson for believing in me.

Without each of you, this work would not be.

Thank you.

PREFACE

Catholicism is a spiritual superpower that has shaped the history of the western world. The Catholic Church, like any large and complex organization, is not without its internal controversies, nor is it free of scandal. One such controversy is celibacy among priests. This issue has been debated for most of the nearly two thousand years of the Church's existence, during which it has accumulated great wealth and revealed many gaps between religious doctrine and practice.

The Catholic priesthood did not begin as a celibate establishment. According to the Gospels, many of the Apostles had wives. Early Popes were commonly married and eleven subsequent popes were sons of popes or clergy. Beginning in 500 A.D. married priests took advantage of members of the Church and willed Church land to their children. Soon the Church, in order to insure its own growth and lands, forbid descendants of priests to inherit Church-owned property.

In the 11th century Pope Gregory VII prohibited all married priests from saying mass and forbade all parishioners from attending masses said by them. The first law actually forbidding priests to marry was handed down in 1139 at the Second Latern Council. Since then, six popes have sired fifteen illegitimate children, all after 1139 A.D.

More recently, clerical celibacy, or lack thereof, has been related to many, if not most, of the scandals that have occurred in the past couple of decades. Sadly, the worst examples of such scandals were realized when an extensive history of child sexual abuse was exposed with staggering statistics.

In the beginning, these pedophiliac priests were not defrocked or purged from the ranks. Instead, they were protected by being transferred to another parish that was unlikely to be aware of the controversy. In an excerpt from the *Annals of Religion: Cold Sanctuary, "How The Church Lost Its Mission"*, published in the June 12, 2002 edition of The New Yorker, Thomas Keneally wrote:

The proliferating reports of pedophilia among the clergy have been devastating enough; perhaps even more disturbing have been the evasive responses by such Church leaders as Cardinal Bernard Law, of Boston. For them, it has been business as usual; a pity about the few bad eggs and, of course, the victims must take their share of the blame, too.

Under a disciplinary code adopted by the U.S. bishops during that same year, it appeared that priests accused of sexually abusing minors were to be publicly identified. The process had begun. Some were removed from the ministry and assigned to a life of prayer and penance; some have been stripped of all their priestly duties while others have simply faded into the woodwork, somewhere, perhaps awaiting their destiny.

It may come as no surprise then that priests who father children are not subject to any significant censure---unless of course they marry. Accurate statistics with regard to Catholic priests fathering children are difficult to obtain, if they exist at all. It has been noted, however, that some modern-day priests have been heard making reference to the rectory in which they live as a "home for unwed fathers."

It takes an egregious abuse of power and trust for these priests to fulfill their forbidden desires. Equally as troubling is the fact that the Church preaches charity, yet often lacks it when it comes to these women and their children. Very often they are ostracized and plagued as women of "low" and questionable character. Some are bribed for their silence. Seldom, however, are they viewed as victims. Most are seen as predators and publicly shamed. Perhaps the next public crisis that awaits the Church is the revelation of the cruel abuse of these women by religious leaders and the insensitive responses of the Church hierarchy.

The real shame is that many of the children born of priests seldom have the chance of ever knowing their biological fathers or the history of their ancestry. From the very beginning, an infant is robbed of a family heritage because, in so many cases, the father remains forever anonymous.

As to the degree of paternal support, if any at all, it seldom rivals the cost of raising a child. More fortunate families are provided the basic financial support required by law. Some priests secretly maintain ongoing relationships, while hiding from the Church and community, subsequently subjecting these families to tremendous social pressures. Other families are simply broken, shunned, and left to fend for themselves.

The Church has a reputation of moral leadership to protect. That results in a strategy that aims at hiding the priest and covering up his behaviors. From the beginning of the Church those who become ordained priests are regarded as having been elevated to positions of trust and in God's grace. Because this belief still remains today, it is essential for the Church to vigorously guard men of the cloth even if it means the need to conceal, destroy, or deny evidence that contradicts public perception and expectation.

Some believe the Catholic Church is systematically eroding its credibility as a moral leader. While it continues to portray lofty ideas of purity, chastity, respect for human and family life, and forgiveness, it has supported clergy who have failed to embrace these ideals---clergy who have committed acts that run contrary to the Church's own basic teachings.

Abortion is a polarizing subject in America. The Catholic Church has taken a firm, unwavering stance against this process, stating that its position is a non-negotiable moral absolute that is never to be altered.

The Catholic Church has always condemned abortion as a grave evil. Christian writers, from the first century to Pope John Paul II in his encyclical *Evangelium Vitae* (The Gospel of Life), has maintained that the Bible forbids abortion, just as it forbids murder.

Thus, in 1995 Pope John Paul II declared that the Church's teaching on abortion:

...is unchanged and unchangeable. Therefore, by the authority which Christ conferred upon Peter and his successors---I declare that direct abortion, that is, abortion willed as an end or as a means, always constitutes a grave moral disorder, since it is the

deliberate killing of an innocent human being. This doctrine is based upon the natural law and upon the written word of God, is transmitted by the Church's tradition and taught by the ordinary and universal magisterium.

No circumstance, no purpose, no law whatsoever can ever make licit an act which is intrinsically illicit, since it is contrary to the law of God which is written in every human heart, knowable by reason itself, and proclaimed by the Church.

The question that needs to be asked is this: Has there been an unwritten addendum added to this moral dogma of the Church making it permissible to take the life of an unborn child if that means protecting the Church's infallibility and moral authority over personal human behavior?

What you are about to read is a true story of the human suffering that resulted from the hypocrisy of the Catholic Church and the true costs of its unyielding and dispassionate self-serving treatment of others.

This is my story…

CHAPTER 1

I sat with my slender legs dangling over the edge of the gurney with its stiff, white linen tucked neatly beneath me, wondering how I got there. I was having unusual thoughts taking me way back to my beginning. My birth mother had given me up for adoption. Thank heaven she made the choice to give me life. As a result, I was adopted and raised as an only child by a wonderful, French Catholic family. I wondered if she ever thought of having an abortion. Suddenly all of that didn't seem to matter; not with what I was about to do. But why was I doing this? I truly believed in the sacredness of life, and I was so happy to be pregnant. Why then, was I sitting here waiting to have an abortion?

I love Matthew so—but do I love him so much that I am willing to take the life of our baby? Thoughts were swirling wildly through my head. I want to see my child walk and play and go to college some day. I want this baby. So, why am I here? Why am I sitting here in this place with bright lights, cold steel and the unrelenting, pungent odor of disinfectant? I can't, I just can't do this! How did I get here?

I knew that it all started the night that Matthew took me to meet that minister. I don't remember his name, but his office was in a long, white, portable trailer that sat on the boundary line of a parking lot. He was a big man with a warm smile. He looked at me as though I was a vulnerable little lamb, quite insignificant, being safely herded by my shepherd. Although the reason for the meeting was all about me and our baby, I was never invited to enter into the conversation. He and Matthew exchanged words, made plans. The minister placed a phone call—I don't remember what was said, but I'm certain now that the conversation was all about my being there, on that gurney, that day. I cringed. I felt my hands gripping the side of the gurney so tightly that it was cutting into my palms.

Wait a minute! Why is this all happening? I thought. Is it because having this baby would mean that the sterling reputation of the Church stands to be tarnished? Or, is it that a priest has broken his promise of obedience to his bishop as well as his vow of celibacy and soon everyone will know it? Actually, it's both. In minutes, the life of this baby that I am carrying is scheduled to be terminated. This abortion has been arranged by a priest; it is supported by the Church. How right is that? How right is it to take the life of an innocent infant to protect the reputation of a Catholic priest?

It was all coming together. The reality of what was happening made sense. The very Church whose doctrine on abortion was a very clearly defined stance opposing the taking of the life of a baby from the moment of conception was now willing to compromise that position. I was about to destroy the evidence that showed the shortcomings of one of its perfect men. Perhaps an exception written in small print should be an addendum to this doctrine, with the following: "Alter only if the birth of this child will bring forth public knowledge of a clergyman's imperfections, thereby tarnishing his reputation, position and moral authority." The bottom line: If there is no child, there is no threat.

The stakes were high, too high…so, at all costs, the order was given to do whatever was necessary to erase any and all evidence that this perfect man had fallen—making certain that in so doing, he remained totally unscathed.

Thoughts continued to whirl in my head. "No…no…no." I began to cry. Confused, sick to my stomach, heartbroken, I looked around. There were white walls, white lights, white linen, white everything. Ironic that I was surrounded by the very color that symbolizes purity. Quickly lunging for the basin, I vomited.

The nurse didn't seem flustered with my discomfort. She took the filled basin from me as she said, "The doctor will be in shortly. The doctor will be in shortly," she repeated.

"I don't want any doctor to be in shortly!" I cried out, "I'm not going through with this. I want to have my baby!"

The nurse ignored my reaction as she glided across the short distance that separated us, never saying a word to me.

"But you don't understand...I won't do it," my voice was pleading.

No response.

Speaking more loudly I continued, "I won't do it. I won't do it."

"Did she hear me this time?" I asked myself.

I persisted, determined, now, not to be dismissed. As she was walking around me I said, "You heard me didn't you? You heard me?"

Placing her hand on my shoulder, she said, "Dear, I know you're frightened. Maybe you really want this baby, but you can't think of just yourself at a time like this; you also have to consider what the baby's father wants. He seems pretty set with his decision." And she walked away.

Heaven forbid that I become insensitive to the wishes of my baby's father. Why should his wellbeing even enter my mind. Matthew is waiting somewhere in the outer chambers of this white room. I really don't care what or how he is doing right now. He certainly hasn't appeared concerned about my feelings all along. As I lay awake all last night he slept like a baby. He also wasn't a bit distracted this morning; he drank his coffee and read the paper while I cried. My well-being wasn't on his mind even then. Now I'm told that I should be thinking about what he wants?

I was scared. I was so scared as I sat on this god-forsaken gurney. My heart was breaking at the thought of having my baby's life terminated. On the other hand, Matthew was most likely comfortably situated in the waiting room, probably feeling pretty invulnerable in that in his mind, the evidence showing his infidelity to his bishop and to the Church will soon be destroyed. Then for him, everything will return to normal. For me, it will never be the same; and for my baby, it will never be at all. How and why did I ever allow myself to reach this point? And Matthew, the Church—how can this even be real?"

Moments...moments after having those thoughts I felt as though I had catapulted off that gurney. Before my feet touched the floor I had ripped off the hospital gown and was reaching for my clothes. I dressed quickly. Almost immediately, I heard the metal hooks scraping on the metal rod which held the white curtain that separated my tiny stall from the large room. The sound of the curtain being slid open was like fingernails on a chalkboard. There stood the doctor dressed in scrubs—the same man that Matthew and I had met a little earlier.

This time he appeared somewhat less sensitive than when I was initially introduced to him. News travels fast. In a rather robotic fashion, he recited the everyone-goes-through-this routine line in an attempt to encourage me to reconsider. The more he spoke, the more strength and courage I gained. I think that I now know how David felt when he slew Goliath. Nothing, and absolutely no one, was going to stand in my way. I bravely and clearly articulated that the decision to carry my baby to term was final. So, I was ready to leave.

"If you're determined not to go through this, you have details to attend to before you leave," the doctor said, as he abruptly turned and walked away.

"You must have an exit interview with our social worker," murmured the nurse who had suddenly appeared out of nowhere, "and of course, your boyfriend must be there with you. You need to explain to him why you have changed your mind."

So be it. Let's get this interview over with, was the silent answer milling in my head but the response I verbalized was simply, "Fine."

I wondered if this woman thought that she would intimidate me by throwing in the "the boyfriend must be there" bit. No, I repeatedly said to myself, no. The well-being of my baby is and will remain my one and only focus.

Still in the process of buttoning my blouse, I could feel the pressure of a hand on my back pushing me forward.

"Excuse me, I would like to get my purse, please," I said in a voice that certainly reflected someone on a mission. I resisted the push that had turned into a gentle shove as I reached under the gurney.

"Hurry girl," demanded the nurse, "We have women waiting who are serious about being here. We need to take care of them, so let's move along."

"No problem," I said, "no problem—anymore."

She led me through a large white room that was divided by stalls such as the one that I had just left. I could only see into three of the dozen or so cubicles. The curtains were open and the gurneys were empty. The door that we were heading toward was at the opposite end from where I had entered. I was escorted into an office, but not the same room in which the intake interview had been held. It was a small, dull, smoky-beige, stuffy room with tiny windows and dirty-looking, brownish gray curtains. It had an old wooden desk in one corner, folding chairs, no pictures on the walls and nothing to personalize the space. The smell was terrible, stale as though the air had been motionless forever. It certainly wasn't an environment that had been decorated to radiate a warm, safe and caring atmosphere. There was no way to counter the message that this space gave. Everything was very different from what I had experienced in the bright, very comfortable office where the intake procedure had taken place earlier that morning.

As I entered, the social worker was sitting behind the desk, and Matthew was coming in through the door on the opposite side of the room. "They must have two separate offices," I thought, "and the nature of the business determines which room is used." This was the least desirable of the two, but then I didn't represent a model patient.

Needless to say, this was not a supportive meeting. It was scripted, cold and matter of fact. Before I had a chance to sit down, the social worker had started in.

"Many women going through this get cold feet. Given a little time, the nervousness works its way out, the procedure is done and women leave happy with their decision of having done what was in the best interest of everyone." She continued, "It's quite obvious that you've made up your mind and you're not willing to give yourself that extra time. I suggest that you simply explain to er..." she quickly glanced down at her file, "Matthew—do tell Matthew why you've decided not to have this scheduled procedure."

Matthew, taken totally by surprise, turned toward me with a scowl on his brow and his piercing blue eyes darting toward me like I'd never seen before.

"I'm not going through with the abortion, Matthew. I'd like to leave now."

Without skipping a beat, he said in a stern, chilling voice, "I certainly don't understand this behavior. Kate, going through with this termination is such an easy solution, and we're right here. Why are you being so selfish and thinking only of yourself? You know having the procedure would be best for both of us."

I said nothing.

"If you don't have the abortion, do you realize what that will do to me? What will I tell the--" He stopped without completing the sentence. I could have filled in the blank.

I knew why he just couldn't bring himself to say that last word in front of the social worker. It would have exposed his identity as a Roman Catholic priest. He obviously didn't want to do that, but then, it wasn't Matthew's style to leave a tale untold. As he searched for words, I chose to simplify and expedite matters. So, I stood up, leaned toward him and softly whispered:

"Papa, don't preach."

That totally disengaged Matthew's aggressiveness. He didn't fall off the chair, but a simple touch of a feather would have helped him do just that. I was gaining momentum by the minute and there was no stopping me now. Since they were both sitting, I towered over them as I reached across the desk and picked up the file folder that was lying there. I checked to make certain that my name was printed on the label. Once confirmed, I proceeded to tear the folder in half. I nonchalantly and quite arrogantly dropped the two pieces onto Matthew's lap, turned on my heels and walked toward the door. Looking back and directly into his eyes, I said:

"Matthew, it's not over, my darling—it's really just begun."

CHAPTER 2

O nce through the door, I stepped into a poorly-lighted hall-way that had two doors. One door had a sign on the glass that read:

No Admittance—Restricted Area—Employees Only

The other had an exit sign over it.

This must be the hidden part of the building, I thought. Were all women who had a change of heart escorted out through this back door instead of going out through the waiting room? Could it be that the women who were waiting were being spared the sight of those of us who had changed our minds? Holding back an out-burst of emotions, my pace increased as I headed toward the exit sign. I swung open the door and walked out onto a very narrow back alley.

There were barrels with trash bags everywhere and two dump-sters at the end of the building. I didn't even want to think of what these people considered trash. A wired fence lined the entire length of the building, and the windows had wrought-iron bars in them. I just couldn't get out fast enough—the path seemed to go on for miles.

Finally, I reached the end of the building. Taking a long, deep breath, I fully expected to break down and burst into tears. The past few weeks had been so mentally, physically and emotionally draining. Strangely enough, I didn't shed a tear. Instead, I felt an amplifying surge of freedom. I placed my hands over my belly, raised my eyes to the heavens and whispered:

"From now on, it's just you and me, Babe." That was the very moment that marked the true beginning of a lifelong relationship that would exist between my baby and me.

Although it was a cold March day in New York, somehow the

J. C. Soucier

rays of the sun connected with my proudly pregnant body, wrapping me into a very warm, cuddly hug. It felt so good. It made me feel strong, even invincible.

Suddenly, I knew that I had a purpose. I had been given a very precious gift; I was willing to devote my life to the health, well-being and success of this child that I had co-created. From this moment on, we became a team.

At some point in the middle of this daydream, I felt a hand on my arm. It was Matthew, and without a word, he gently directed me toward the parking lot where the car was parked. A perfect gentleman, he had always opened doors for me, but not this time. He went directly to his side of the vehicle. I opened my own door and sat down. He slid into his seat and in a chilling tone of voice said quite loudly:

"I don't know what you think you're trying to prove by doing this, Kate. Not only are you absolutely wrong, but you embarrassed me. There'll be many consequences to your actions, wait and see. You cost me over $500 because they wouldn't refund my fee. Thanks. How will I explain this?"

Quite confused, I couldn't imagine what he was talking about. Who would he have to explain this to? Was it to the bishop back in our home state? Did he know of my pregnancy? Aside from the two of us, my doctor at home knew that I was pregnant. The minister who was the middle man and made the arrangements for the abortion knew. Those at the clinic knew. Who else? Why would Matthew owe anyone an explanation?

Did he borrow the money for the car rental, the lavish dinner, the roses, the plush hotel accommodations, the trip itself and the foiled abortion attempt? He paid for it all. Now that the cash was gone and the pregnancy was not—he has to explain this to someone? Who is this someone? Did he get the money from the Church? Could it have been from the bishop himself? Was it Your Excellency himself who would need an explanation? Did the Church really sponsor this plan?

Shaking my head slightly, I tried to bring things back into perspective. I was oddly willing to let the events of the morning go in trade for just a little peace. After what had happened today, why would I be concerned about whom Matthew needs to face? Could it be because I love him so? We had chosen two different paths. Now, in a single car, on the same long highway, we were returning to two separate worlds. Alone, we would have to face the demons that awaited each of us. I was willing and ready to do whatever needed to be done because maintaining the health and well-being of my baby was primary on my mind.

As for Matthew, he would run back to the environment that he knew best. There, he would find protection like so many others had before him as well as those who would follow for decades to come. From that point on, it will be business as usual. Day after day, Matthew will continue to make his entrance from the sanctuary to the altar garbed in colorful symbolic vestments (the alb representing purity and innocence) and celebrate mass. No one will be the wiser.

CHAPTER 3

Only twenty minutes of travel time behind us and already it seemed like hours. It was so long...so silent. I thought again about the demons that awaited Matthew and those that I would have to face.

The stability of Matthew's position really did not stand to be threatened by my pregnancy; if word should get out, he'd simply be transferred to another parish and go on pretending that nothing had happened. He would never have to worry about having a roof over his head, having food on the table or paying bills. Sooner or later, however, Matthew would have to come face-to-face with his demon...or would he?

My situation was somewhat different. Oh, I had a roof over my head because I had been living with and caring for my aging mother since the death of my dad. I put the food on the table, paid the bills, including the salary of a full time housekeeper-companion, and I also worked full time as a high school teacher.

The playing field seemed a little unfair—in 1972, a single woman who was pregnant was not exactly a candidate for citizen of the year, nor was being a member of the teaching staff at the local public high school deemed appropriate.

I decided that I would say nothing for now and as soon as the school year ended, I would submit my letter of resignation. Not being employed would certainly present its challenges. Fortunately, I'd been teaching for seven years and had managed to save some money. I knew that I would continue being paid through the summer, so that would be helpful. I had also received an inheritance from my dad. All combined, the family's needs would be covered for a few years. It was my hope to be able to manage to stay at home to raise my child during the early years

11

and also to be my mother's primary caregiver. There would be few luxuries, but that was okay because being able to properly provide the basics for my baby and my mother was all that really mattered.

Keeping the pregnancy a secret until June would be difficult since by then I would be in my fifth month of pregnancy. Being athletic and very active had its advantages in that it kept me trim and in very good condition. Hopefully, that would help conceal the miracle that was growing inside me. Once the letter was mailed to the superintendent, I would share the news of expecting this precious baby with my mother first, then with my Aunt Julia (my mothers' sister) and with my best friend, Jeanne. After that, I would tell my other friends.

I turned toward Matthew, hoping with all my heart that the solitude in travel had given him the opportunity to rethink, reconsider the nature and reasons for my actions. Maybe, just maybe, he could now better understand and support my decision. It didn't happen. The tranquility that I was feeling was almost surreal. It defied Matthew's chilling vibrations that resounded in the car.

Have I lost Matthew forever? Was he really ever mine? The other woman was the Church. Where did I ever get the idea that I would win that war? Or did I ever think of it as a war? Was it more of a period of time that had been extracted from reality just to show me what true love really is? Did I accidentally end up with the jewel of all treasures by becoming pregnant? I won...I wasn't out to win or lose but as it happened...I won.

Matthew and I had shared many conversations about my falling in love with a priest, feeling responsible for his breaking his vow of celibacy and where this relationship was headed. Nothing was ever resolved; we simply fell deeper and deeper in love.

"I was a man long before I became a priest," was Matthew's standard response. He never wavered from it.

Since I didn't take issue with his answer, the questions remained just that, questions. The facts were known from the very beginning. It was a no-win situation and the relationship was on a collision course. Turn and walk away, Kate...turn and walk away, Matthew. We both heard these words being whispered to us from within. Neither of us listened.

We ignored our responsibilities. The evident danger of our choice encouraged the intensity of this relationship to grow. Our love blossomed as the summer days that we spent together became more and more frequent. It was almost like the inappropriateness of our relationship fueled it and made it that much more passionate. The question that neither Matthew nor I ever wanted to entertain or discuss was: How long could this intense fire burn?

CHAPTER 4

The inside of the car was damp and cold, in spite of the sun beaming through the windows. I was feeling as though I'd been riding for hours. I tried to sleep to forget what had just happened, but my thoughts kept going back to that awful white room. Thinking back was very painful, I needed to escape.

I was beginning to relax a little, which led me to wander back in thought to when Matthew and I first met. Those were such happy memories, and I couldn't help but smile.

I taught in a community about twenty miles west of where I lived. I had a habit of stopping off at my cousin Jeanne's home nearly every afternoon just to have coffee, chat and keep in the family loop. Jeanne was not only a relative but also my best friend. She was a nurse and a very gentle, warm, loving mother of three sons. Her husband, Bob, was a post office employee who appeared to be a fun-loving, host-with-the-most sort of guy, the life of the party.

Bob was the pillar of the local Catholic Church, a member of the Diocesan Board of Directors and he served on the Parish Council and other religious connected committees. Jeanne was the President of the Ladies of St. Ann's Sodality and involved in several other professional committees.

Unknown to anyone at that time, her extra-curricular activities were restricted by her very jealous husband. In the eyes of everyone, Bob and Jeanne were a perfect couple, wonderful parents to their children, with a family life that was envied by many.

They had a circle of friends comprised of four other couples and several priests. The common thread that ran amongst them all was that they all loved a good party, good food and lots of laughter. They gathered nearly every Saturday night and celebrated life.

J. C. Soucier

It was July 16, 1969, and a beastly hot evening. I was leaving for Europe the next day with two friends, Janice Thompson and Sarah Snow. Janice, a nurse working in Boston, was a skiing buddy. Sarah was one of my housemates.

Jeanne and Bob were having a barbecue with their group of friends as a little Bon Voyage celebration in my honor. I happened to be sitting across from my cousin at the picnic table in the backyard when suddenly this shiny, impeccably clean gold Oldsmobile pulled up into the driveway. Out jumped a red-headed fellow in khaki shorts and a white T-shirt, carrying a bag containing a bottle of wine and a loaf of French bread. With a huge smile on his face, he called out that he'd be right over. He was on his way into the house to drop off his package. Moments later, he came bouncing out the back door and headed in our direction.

"Kate," said Jeanne, "I'd like to have you meet Father Matt." His name was actually Matthew, but the younger parishioners referred to him as Father Matt, so it stuck for all ages. He extended his hand and I couldn't help but notice that in spite of a strong grip, his skin was soft and snowy white with nicely manicured nails. He certainly did not have the hands of a man who labored.

"Just call me Omar," he said.

"Omar?" I responded. "And why would I call you Omar?"

"For Omar Sharif. Don't you think there's a strong resemblance?"

Whew…that's quite an assumption for him to make, I thought to myself, although he really was quite handsome. It turns out that Father Matt was an avid moviegoer, whimsical by nature and somewhat flamboyant and dramatic in his ways. This response was certainly within his character. He drew laughs from all those around him, which just encouraged this behavior.

He continued to laugh and joke casually throughout the evening. Being of French descent, he was proud to integrate French into his speech, which he did, often. He was charismatic, magnetic, animated, and very, very humorous. People were drawn to him like magnets.

He was so at ease with his power over people that he could sit astride a kitchen chair, sipping a beverage and partaking in a conversation with folks of all ages, denominations and colors while maintaining dignity and command that were palatable to all present. The buzz was that he was destined for a leadership role in the Church. He was widely adored by the parishioners and a respected member of his clerical band. People of all ages loved his sermons; one might say that experience, rather than books, had been his teacher. He just had a way with words.

As the evening progressed, the party games commenced. Since all the others had arrived in pairs, Father Matt and I were teamed up for games such as ping-pong and badminton. From the very beginning, we were a good fit and fared well in challenges, setting the stage for what was to come.

The evening moved along nicely. Suddenly, Bob climbed to stand on the picnic table in attempt to get everyone's attention. He announced that we were but moments away from Apollo 11's blast off. Everyone, anxious to witness this historical event in the making rushed into the house. Gathered around the kitchen table, we all made a lunge to dunk our steak tips into the fondue dish filled with sizzling oil, gather other goodies, and find a ringside seat to watch the launch. The missile was scheduled to land on the moon on July 20, 1969. I knew that I would be in Switzerland on that day, but I never realized until then how great it felt to be an American.

The evening ended with everyone having had a grand time, bulging with patriotic pride, and full to the brim. The next morning, Janice and Sarah picked me up and we headed for the airport en route to board our flight to Munich, Germany.

The memory of the party faded rapidly as my mind was assaulted by the excitement of visiting five foreign and very intriguing countries. Weeks passed. Germany, Austria, Switzerland, England and France each were providing such wonderful and unique experiences. Never looking back, I was thinking of no one in particular as I was very focused and enjoying this trip.

On one particular day all three of us were browsing through a gift shop in Paris when I happened to see a large postcard that was a photograph of Omar Sharif. I had a flashback of Father Matt's response when I met him. Laughing to myself, I removed the card from the rack and added it to my purchases. Since I had no idea where Father Matt lived, I mailed my greeting card from France to him in care of Jeanne. It wasn't until several years later did I discover that the postcard had never reached its intended destination.

CHAPTER 5

W
e returned home from our European jaunt only days before the opening of school. The routine of my daily half
hour commute from Brunswick to Lewiston began again.
Aside from visiting my parents, the extent of my social life in my
home town was stopping at Jeanne's two or three times a week.
Occasionally, Father Matt would drop in and join our impromptu
coffee klatch. Unexpected visits from him apparently were common happenings. He was an extremely unpredictable and spontaneous person who would seldom go by a friend's home without
stopping—"expect him when you see him" seemed to be the short
description of him.

It was Columbus Day and the three musketeers, Kay, my
other housemate, Sarah and I had just returned from having
brunch with friends. I had just nestled in comfortably with a
good book and cup of tea when the phone rang. I reached over,
picked up the phone and much to my surprise heard a familiar
voice. It was Father Matt.

"I have to give a speech at the Ladies of St. Ann's Sodality
meeting on Thursday. Jeanne tells me that you're quite the writer
and I'm really struggling with what to say. I wonder if you would
help me put something together?"

"Absolutely!" I responded. "Why don't you stop by my office
at school—anytime after two o'clock? I'd be more than happy to
help."

"Thank you, Kate. I knew I could count on your help. Better
yet, what do you say I just drop by your house and we could work
on it there?"

"That would be okay, but I live in Brunswick." My home was
twenty miles from Lewiston where Father Matt lived. Distance

was obviously not a deterrent because he was not dissuaded by the information.

He persisted, "That's not a problem. How do I get there?"

I gave him directions and we hung up. I shared the information of company coming with my housemates and they were thrilled to have the opportunity to meet this man whom I had occasionally spoken about and referenced as Omar.

Father Matt arrived early on that cool October night. The foliage was still very visible and burning with brilliant reds, orange and gold. I opened the door before he'd stepped foot onto the porch and welcomed him. He was dressed in his usual clerical garb, a black suit, black shirt and white collar. Upon entering, he sat at the kitchen table and accepted an invitation to have a cup of coffee. A quick call to Kay and Sarah and they were front and center immediately, ready to meet this new friend.

Father Matt jumped in with both feet and invited them to join us. For a stranger, he was mighty familiar—it was his way. He proceeded to entertain all of us for the next several hours. Before I knew it, the three of us were standing on the porch in the chill autumn air waving goodbye to our guest. This had been the first time that I had ever interacted with Father Matt outside of my cousin's home. The experience was fun. After closing the front door, latching it locked and turning off the porch light, I turned to notice a mischievous smile on Kay's face.

"Did you notice anything odd about Father Matt's visit, Kate?" she questioned.

Absolutely clueless, I answered, "No. Why, did you?"

"Tell me," said Kay, "why did Father Matt come again?"

"He came to have me help him write a speech."

"And…did you?"

"Er—why, no." I answered. "Now that you mention it. We never did get to doing that, did we?" Coming to an abrupt but somewhat impish stop, I replayed the events of the evening in my head and soon realized that we had become so wrapped up in Father Matt's entertaining ways that neither of us gave thought to the purpose of his visit. So, the speech went unwritten. I was certain that I would either receive a follow-up call regarding our forgetfulness or meet with Father Matt at Jeanne's within the next day or two.

That didn't happen. It was nearly a full week before I saw Father Matt at Jeanne's. He made no mention of the speech nor did I. Strangely enough, from that time on, we seemed to meet almost daily for afternoon coffees and chats. Totally innocent with absolutely no agenda, I did not realize that these opportunities were developing familiarity between us to the point where we got pretty good at second-guessing each other and even completing one another's sentences.

I had experienced a divorce earlier that year. It had followed a two-year marriage to a man who was unfaithful just after we were engaged. It was nice to have a friend like Father Matt. It seemed like he carried no baggage and was not looking for anything from me other than friendship. Furthermore, the fact that he was a Roman Catholic priest felt safe for me; I would have a male friend without complications or expectations. Such a relationship was so reassuring. I grew to trust and respect him for who he was and what he represented.

CHAPTER 6

I opened my eyes and looked at my watch. Matthew and I had been on the road back to Maine for nearly two hours. Not a word had been spoken between us since we left New York. That was okay; it really had to be okay. Grateful for the chance to retreat into my quiet space and reminisce, I returned to my happy thoughts.

I remembered the very first time Father Matt and I were together alone. It was the evening that we went to the movies. Actually, the only time we ever went to a movie. I'll never forget his call. It was smooth...

"Hi Kate, what are you doing tonight?"

"No plans, why?" I responded.

"I see that *Bob & Carol & Ted & Alice* is playing at your theater. I really want to see that movie. It's getting great ratings. Interested in joining me?"

"Sure. Is that the one with Natalie Wood, Robert Culp, Elliott Gould and Dyan Cannon?"

"Yes, how about it?"

"Sure, sounds like fun."

"I'll be there shortly after five. See you then." And that was it. A quick goodbye— the plan was in motion.

I can still see him coming through the door late that winter afternoon with lay clothes draped over his arm.

"Do you mind if I use your bathroom to change?" he asked as he made his way to the bathroom. Moments later he appeared totally transformed into a man—a very handsome man. Not what I had expected, but then, had I really expected anything?

Although he was a giant of a man in peoples' eyes, Father Matt stood a little over five feet, seven inches and weighed about one hundred, forty-five pounds. His reddish hair was loosely curled and complemented his fair complexion and contagious smile. The gold-rimmed glasses magnified his sparkling, ice-blue eyes.

Noticing these things for the first time was strange. I wondered if the collar was sort of a shield. Was this white stripe around his neck so magical that it deflected temptation for one's eyes to roam? If so, it worked.

Spontaneously, Father Matt asked, "Any good place to eat here in Brunswick? What do you say we get a bite to eat before the movie? We have plenty of time."

"Sounds like a plan," was my usual response to any unexpected, yet appealing invitation that came my way.

"I hear that the Stowe House is very nice. Does that sound good to you?

"Sure," I answered, and with that, we were off.

The Stowe House was where Harriet Beecher Stowe wrote *Uncle Tom's Cabin*. Just being in the restaurant that was housed within the very place where this avant-garde author lived was very exciting to me. To add to this evening of surprises, Andrew Wyeth, world-renowned artist who just happened to be at the top of my list of favorites, entered the room where we were sitting. He and his wife were escorted to the table diagonally across from us! "This will be a highlight of nights to remember," I thought…the gathering of la crème de la crème.

It was sort of like being on a carousel ride surrounded by many of the people who in some way were meaningful to me. Definitely these included Harriet Beecher Stowe, Andrew Wyeth and Father Matt.

Dinner was delicious…and fun. We exchanged stories of life experiences. By the time we left the restaurant it was as if we had been in each other's lives forever. This is where it all began; it was the start of a relationship that was never intended to be.

By the time we entered the theater the weather had started to change; the forecast was snow. After the movie, the evening had turned into a beautiful, magical starlit night covered with a coat of that fresh white stuff. What a sight—very bright white, crisp, unadulterated snow. It was truly a perfect night from beginning to end.

CHAPTER 7

As we walked toward the car, I invited the gently falling snowflakes to land ever so delicately on my outstretched arm.

"How absolutely beautiful" I whispered, "I love to watch snowflakes slowly float to the ground."

"Let's," said Father Matt. "How about we go watch from your cottage? It's not but a few miles away, right?"

Father Matt's knowledge about the location of my cottage led me to believe that, at some point, Jeanne must have mentioned to him the property that overlooked a harbor in Casco Bay. He was right that it was located just a few miles from the town of Brunswick.

"And so, shall we go to your cottage?" asked Father Matt.

"Sure…we're only seven miles away—give or take a few feet."

"Let's go. I'd love to see it."

I had no problem with taking him to see the cottage, although we would be at a bit of a disadvantage. Seeing a brown log cabin in the dark could be challenging.

"I don't have the key with me and the only light will be natural light, no street lights you know. Actually, it boils down to the stars and the moon. How much you'll truly see is debatable. Still want to go?"

"Certainly do. It's such a beautiful night; my headlights will lead the way. Let's jump into this adventure!" So, jump in I did—and off to Blackstone we headed.

Within minutes we had reached the road that led to my summer home. Virgin snow made staying in the middle of this primitive, narrow dirt road a bit of a challenge especially since the majestic Atlantic Ocean that slapped against the rocky coast of Maine was at the foot of the cliff that was but a few feet from the roadway.

There it was—a small brown log cabin sitting innocently in the middle of a soft, white blanket surrounded by beautiful pine trees trimmed in white. Father Matt stopped his car in the middle of the road and opened his door. He came around the car, opened my door and I followed in his footsteps as we headed towards it.

As I looked at the silhouette of the log cabin, I had a clear view of the huge front porch. This had always been my spot of preference even growing up. Memories of my childhood started dancing in my head. I could see the swing that my dad had hung on the porch for me. He would spend hours telling me stories as I would rhythmically swing back and forth.

This was the very spot where my dad told me details about my adoption. It was a beautiful August morning and we had just returned from our morning swim across the bay. I was twelve years old and earlier that spring I had been told by a schoolmate that I had been adopted. Totally in the dark about what the word "adopted" meant, I had come home from school and asked my mother if I had been adopted. Having caught her a little off guard, she calmly responded, "Wait until your father comes home, dear, and we'll talk about it then."

I waited. My dad barely had time to open the door when I launched my question at him. He hugged me and led me into the family room. He sat in his big leather chair while I sat on the oversized leather ottoman at his knees. He took both my hands, held them within his, squeezed them ever so gently and kissed them. He looked up at me through his icy blue eyes and softly said,

"Baby, your mother and I wanted a little girl so very much. We were blessed with the opportunity to choose the one we wanted. We went to a special place, saw many babies and from all of them, we picked you. That makes us very lucky and you very special."

Although I knew there was more to tell, that's all I needed—at that time.

The following summer however, my curiosity had peaked. I was swinging and he was having a fresh cup of coffee. The moment had come to ask for details.

"Daddy" I said, "tell me about my adoption…"

Perfect

"I am happy and proud to tell you about your adoption, Baby, and here's how the story goes. You see, your mother and I so wanted a little girl, and giving birth biologically was not possible for us. Fortunately, adoption was another way that we could have a little girl that we both wanted. There are in this world, very unselfish, wonderful women who, although they give birth to a baby, recognize that they are not in a position to properly care for this child so they take their babies to a place called an orphanage. These are very nice homes where babies are properly cared for until couples like your mother and I are fortunate enough to be referred to them. We were blessed with the opportunity to choose a special child and make her ours. That process is called adoption. That's what we did. A wonderful Lewiston Dominican priest, Fr. Damien from Sts. Peter and Paul Church led us to Holy Innocents' Home on Mellon Street in Portland which is where you were. The minute I saw you, I knew you were the one. Your mother and I didn't hesitate for one single second. The hard part was that we couldn't take you home with us that very day. We had to wait for final papers to be signed by your birth mother. And so we waited. We waited nearly a whole month. When that call finally came and Sister Consolata's soft voice said, "Your daughter will be waiting for you tomorrow," I jumped for joy! We were at the doorstep of Holy Innocents' Home to pick you up at seven o'clock on the morning of Saturday, July 8, 1944. It's a day that I'll never forget; it will always be the best day of my life!"

And so, that's how it all began, and I will forever be grateful to my birth mother for loving me so much.

I so miss that swing…because as I grew older, the swing was replaced by a rocking chair and the stories became memories.

Father Matt and I reached the cottage and climbed the steps. Not too long before I had stood on this very same porch with my dad, involved in one of our "this is how we'll save the world" conversations. Now, I was positioned in the same spot with someone new—someone whom I was slowly beginning to trust and enjoy. I believed that this new friend would help me recover from my heartaches and would teach me to love life all over again. No hurt, no fears, no involvement, just loving and living life as it was meant

27

J. C. Soucier

to be…flying kites, wading through puddles while walking in the summer rain, skimming rocks across the water, gathering bouquets of wild flowers, watching minnows swimming energetically in rock wells, watching the tide come in and go out…just another chance to live life as it was meant to be lived.

What a night! The intensity of the light from the full moon made the water sparkle as though it was an ocean of diamonds. The white glistening snow encircled us as though we were within a crystal palace. The beauty was breathtaking and the sound of silence was golden.

Suddenly, the stillness was broken by the sound of footsteps, fast, galloping. A doe, a beautiful little doe was running across the lawn and leaped past us. Like a flash of light she had come and gone; her prints in the snow were the only evidence of her having been there. When the snow melted, her tracks would disappear as would proof that she ever made that crossing. I thought, "One just must believe."

Unable to enter the cottage, Father Matt cupped his hands around his face and placed them against the large front window in an attempt to glimpse what was inside. It was very dark; he couldn't see much so he asked for a verbal description of the layout. I accommodated.

"A kitchen, a bath, a living-dining room, two bedrooms and a loft. Running water, a Franklin fireplace and a natural alarm clock." That was a short but full description of what this humble little cottage by the sea had to offer. But there would be more…

"A natural alarm clock?" Father Matt reiterated.

"Indeed," I responded, "We have very friendly, neighboring squirrels who dance across the rooftop every morning. Their footsteps are loud and clear—it's their way of waking us to make sure that they're fed on schedule. My dad scattered nuts for them every day; and in his absence, I do it. Of course, his generous habit may have encouraged them to bring friends and family, but that was okay. This has become the restaurant of choice for them. I'm sure that they'll live forever. They have plenty of food to eat and equally as much to store for the winter months—believe me!"

"Squirrels? Those are destructive rodents, Kate!" Father Matt

28

exclaimed with a wrinkle in his nose.

"In your eyes perhaps they are, Father Matt, but not in mine. They have never entered our cottage to nest—nor have they been destructive in this neighborhood at all. I'm convinced that they're too smart to bite the hand that feeds them. They know a good thing when they have it. So, God's little creatures live on, full bellies and all!"

Father Matt was silent and smiled as his hand gently patted my back. Was he agreeing or simply giving in to the power of the moment? Without further interaction, we walked back to the car. He opened the door for me and then made his way to the other side, got in and we headed for Brunswick.

I hated to see the evening end. But then, what choices did I have? As we drove into my yard Father Matt said, "Thank you for a wonderful time, Kate; we'll have to do this again very soon. Everything was so perfect."

I returned the compliment and stepped out of his car. From my porch I waved goodbye, unlocked my door and took one final glance before walking in. He was gone and so was the night.

He was right though. It was a perfect time. Since there were no warnings, no clues, who would know then that my cozy summer cottage would become the catalyst, the carousel, the hideaway that would allow the unallowable to happen?

CHAPTER 8

It was several days before Father Matt and I saw one another again. It was at Jeanne's place. Our mutual visit was casual as usual; he arrived shortly after I did and was in high gear—he was on a joke-telling kick where the beginning of the next joke didn't await the punch line of the one he was telling. He certainly provided genuine belly laughter, known to be good for the soul.

The gathering was brief on this particular day. I had errands to run in Brunswick and time was beginning to close in on me. Going out the door, I mentioned that I would be back Saturday afternoon. Since I had a commitment at my folks' in the morning, I'd plan to drop by on the way out of town.

It was a cold, cold Saturday. The season for heavy snow to fall and the temperature to drop to freezing had arrived. Snowmobile enthusiasts were chomping at the bit.

As promised, I swung by Jeanne's before heading out of town. Members of the inner circle had also dropped in for coffee. The inner circle referred to four other couples who habitually gathered with Jeanne and Bob for social encounters. I walked in to find them deep into a conversation that was totally focused on snowmobiling. All the couples had sleds. With lots of snow being predicted for the following week, they were all anxious to begin their Saturday night gatherings at Tacoma Lake just outside of the city. There they would ride long into the night and then wrap up the evening with some indoor social time and refreshments. Anticipation was in the air, and the excitement was contagious.

Right in the middle of this high energy verbal exchange, Father Matt excused himself, saying that he would return shortly. In his absence, the conversation continued. What seemed to be only a few moments later, someone drove into Jeanne and Bob's driveway and was blowing the horn. We all bounced to our feet and ran to the windows to see what the noise was all about. There was Father Matt's gold Oldsmobile towing a brand new trailer that was showcasing a shiny yellow snowmobile. He decided to get in on this fun and purchased his own toy! Father Matt was never one to be outdone by any of his friends. That toy was about to add a whole new dimension to my relationship with him.

A few weeks passed and coffee visits became perpetual. Unintentionally, and with no effort on my part, we continued to nourish our relationship. Then, the big day arrived. The first snowmobile outing was scheduled, and I was invited. I gave up my usual weekend skiing at Sugarloaf and agreed to spend the following Saturday trying out this winter sport. It had been decided that since everyone was doubled up on their sleds, I would go with Father Matt. Not a second thought was given to that assignment; it was just the way it was going to be.

That was okay with everyone, and certainly fine with me. Off to the sled I headed for the maiden ride on this new toy which would be driven by someone who was very adventurous and totally inexperienced. Little did I know how very dangerous this combination would be.

That first experience was a hoot! Father Matt had put in very little time learning to drive and maneuver the heavy sled. He'd been taken out on a few test runs and given basic rules and regulations, but that was about it. No one had thought to advise him to carry spare spark plugs, which seemed to be a basic and frequent need of this particular machine. Even if they had told him to tuck a few in his pocket should the sled choke and stop, he wouldn't have had a clue as to what to do with them.

The time had come. Everyone started their sleds and revved up the motors in anticipation of making the first trip of the season. Our sled was the last of the six on the trail. We sped across the vast, open lake and into the woods. What an unbelievable feeling of freedom! Although very warmly dressed, it wasn't long before I buried my face in Father Matt's jacket, shielding it from the cold air. Being nestled back there added to the comfort that the whole setting had to offer.

Perfect

As the sled weaved in and out between trees and occasionally jumped over a knoll, the only way to stay on that sled was to hang onto Matthew for dear life. I loosened my grip when suddenly the need to hide my face from the cold was no longer necessary. There's no breeze when one is stopped! What a surprise it was to discover how much of a challenge a tiny little part like a spark plug can present. One minute we were riding along a beautiful trail, and the next minute, we were not moving. At that time, Father Matt had absolutely no idea why this sled had come to a sudden stop. There we sat, in what appeared to be the middle of nowhere, just Father Matt, me and the snowmobile.

Our choices were few. We were alone and miles from the base camp. Neither one of us seemed concerned; we both knew that sooner or later, someone would discover that we had dropped from the group and would come back for us. It was just a matter of waiting. Father Matt sputtered a little about having a brand new sled that had malfunctioned first time out. Without a second thought, he stretched out his arms and legs, sighing deeply as he dropped backwards into the deep snow. Little did he realize that he was down for the count because there was so much accumulation of powdered snow along the sides of the trail that he couldn't support himself properly in order to get up. With each attempt his arm would sink deeper and deeper into the snow.

After Father Matt's several unsuccessful, independent attempts to stand up, I extended my hand to help him. Then there were two! Now we were both in the same predicament, prisoners of the wilderness. Our laughter echoed throughout the forest as we couldn't refrain from reacting to the amusing sight of one another. Our glee was interrupted by the arrival of our rescue team.

Once Bob and Jeanne got over the hilarious sight of us buried in snow, they pulled Father Matt and me up on our feet. The spark plug having been changed, within minutes the engine of the sled was roaring and we were merrily on our way once again.

It was a long winter—lots of snow, lots of cold weather. I did very little skiing and a great deal of snowmobiling that year. I was behind Father Matt every Saturday night and on an occasional Sunday afternoon into the evening, the expeditions becoming more and more frequent as the season and snowfalls progressed. I continued feeling very comfortable latching onto his waist and snuggling my face into the back of his jacket. Our antics were ongoing, speeding across the lake, making new trails through the woods, wrestling in the snow and warming up by the fire drinking hot chocolate while others engaged in something a little more spirited. It seemed like a magic time for both of us as we began to realize that we were sharing a genuine, loving friendship. I couldn't help but rejoice at the thought that I felt secure; truly believing that Father Matt would not invade my thoughts or violate my space. He would leave my dreams with all boundaries intact. I had met my soul mate, my perfect friend.

CHAPTER 9

I awoke from my daydream only to read a sign that said, Welcome to Connecticut—that meant that we were still at least four hours from home. I glanced over at Matthew and he was looking straight ahead.

I'm sure that he saw my head turn toward him, but he never reacted. He didn't flinch, his expression didn't alter, nor did he speak a word. Things between us had changed so quickly. Normally, I would have leaned over and lovingly touched him. Today, the thought repulsed me.

Having to make a choice was not in the cards, I thought, at least not from the deck he held. Everything had been so perfect—from the beginning to what I guessed was the end, this morning.

Remaining in the moment was still too difficult and unpleasant for me. I had so many good memories, no need to suffer, I thought to myself. I'll just continue reminiscing about the good times as I slowly let myself drift back to 1970, our first almost full summer together.

The snow had melted, the flowers were blossoming and spring was in the air. The school year had come to an end, and I had moved out to the cottage. My dad suffered a heart attack in late June and was hospitalized. That brought me back home to stay with my mother who suffered from multiple sclerosis. It was just a bit shy of a week when my dad was discharged. He was an extremely active man who didn't enjoy sitting still for very long. The restrictions of being bedridden in a hospital bed and wired up to a monitor were quickly viewed by his doctor as being detrimental to his well-being as opposed to helpful. Therefore, home he came accompanied by very strict orders.

During the initial convalescing period, I stayed at their home.

J. C. Soucier

After the first two weeks I went back to the cottage. I traveled to the city several times a week to refresh groceries and run errands for my folks. Other than that, I spent most of my time out on the water.

By day, I could be found lifting the mainsail or jib on my 30-foot fiberglass sloop, looking forward to carving through the water in silence or enjoying smooth travel on my Carver bridge cruiser. Both had a fully-equipped galley and overnight accommodations for six.

In the evenings, I often enjoyed the company of Lois Frost, a longtime friend who had a cottage on Birch Island which was located across from Blackstone. Lois was an art teacher in the Brunswick school system. She summered on the island and wintered in Brunswick proper. We often spent evenings together sitting on the porch or on the rocks by the water, enjoying the calmness of the bay, picking away at steamed or boiled lobsters, crabs, mussels and clams.

Since a body of water separated our summer homes, cell phones were not in existence in 1970, nor was there electricity or landlines on the island, we had designed our own message system. With the help of binoculars, Lois had a clear view of my porch, so we decided that draping a white beach towel over the banister would be the signal that I was at home. The towel, absent from sight indicated that I was not there. By using this indicator, Lois was certain that the purpose for her crossings would be met. On this particular evening, out went the towel and across came Lois.

We really enjoyed sharing conversations, and this night started out the very same way. We were sitting on the rocking chairs on the porch. The sun had set and the starlit sky was glimmering. The phosphorescence in the water sparkled like diamonds, and the silhouette of a jumping fish could occasionally be seen. In the midst of this beauty, we were interrupted by the headlights of a car coming down the dirt road and, turning into my driveway, heading directly for the porch stairs. The car stopped and I recognized it. The door to this gold Oldsmobile opened and out jumped the driver, pizza in hand.

"I just happened to be in the neighborhood and thought I'd

drop by and share my pizza," were the words that Father Matt announced gleefully. It was certainly a surprise to see him, and more of a surprise to hear why he'd dropped by!

Lois was an extremely intuitive person, and years later she told me how uncomfortable she felt with us that day. Not wanting to appear rude, she recalled working hard to extend her visit a little longer. However, it got the best of her and she finally excused herself, saying that it was getting dark and she needed to cross.

"Need to go, no streetlights lining the length of the bay," she commented in her dry humorous way. Down to the wharf and off to her wooden, flat-bottom boat she went.

Father Matt stayed on for another hour or two, making occasional idle conversation. The silence was comfortable; almost as though we really didn't have to speak to communicate.

"What a little piece of paradise you have, Kate. Being here must be as close to heaven as one would want on earth," he said. Little did we know that those words opened the gate to what was to become a journey into forbidden territory.

CHAPTER 10

Father Matt knew that I was quite well-versed in navigation and that the sea was my second home. Whenever we saw one another, he would speak of his love for the ocean and how very much he wanted to learn the "ways of the sea." It became very clear to me that he was yearning for the day when he would be capable of not only being confident at the helm of a boat but skilled enough to have plotted out his own course. Although not yet formally requested, the writing was on the wall. Someday—somewhere, it was my destiny to teach this man to navigate and sail.

Summer of 1970—it had been nearly one year since Father Matt and I had met. The days were sun-kissed and aromatic. Flowers were blossoming everywhere creating fields of red, yellow, orange and purple like an oversized version of Joseph's coat of many colors.

I had a morning ritual at the cottage that I absolutely loved. Squirrels would wake me about six a.m. and the day began with feeding time at the zoo. From there, I would push the button on the coffee pot that had been prepared the night before. A quick transfer from my nightclothes to my swimsuit and I was off to the wharf and into the water for my morning swim.

Fifteen or twenty minutes later and totally refreshed, I would head toward one of the fields to gather fresh flowers. Bouquet in hand, I would return to the cottage to place the day's pick in a vase on the table, always keeping a few to put in a container to decorate the small corner table on the porch. Meanwhile, the aroma of freshly brewed coffee was in the air, extending a very warm, absolutely irresistible invitation to indulge. After a quick shower, I'd pour myself some coffee, make my way out to the porch, sit in my favorite rocking chair and savor every moment the simplicity of this life had to offer.

Is everything in life free? I would occasionally ask myself out loud. The beautiful, God-given things in life are free. Since nature's simplicity creates beauty within, then everything that really matters in life is free. With that came peace of mind, heart and soul. I just loved my mornings at Blackstone. I shared ever so privately with the birds and occasional squirrel or two. How much more simple and beautiful could life be? It just didn't get much better than that. Or, did it?

Day after day I enjoyed this time. I just treasured the serenity of the morning and the glass-like reflective effect of the sea. No wind, no boat traffic—just calm—and ever so tiny ripples that when combined, would make a difference somewhere, someday. As I was off in my own little world and loving it, the peacefulness and calmness of these precious moments was rudely interrupted by a car coming into my driveway. It wasn't eight o'clock yet and there it was—a gold Oldsmobile parked next to my cottage.

"Hello," was the greeting from Father Matt. "It's going to be much too beautiful a day to spend in the city. I'm hoping that you won't take offense to my taking you to lunch, although there is one string attached."

"Hi," I answered, "and the string is…?"

"That we travel to the restaurant by sea."

"To the restaurant by boat?" I responded, still a little annoyed that my very private and protected intimate morning time had prematurely ended. I wasn't accountable to anyone since my divorce so I was pretty spoiled. When I was at the cottage, I was very particular about what and when I did anything. This wasn't part of the script and yes—I was exasperated. However, I wasn't so irritated that I objected to his suggestion, because I responded to him by saying:

"What a deal!"

By 9:30 Father Matt and I were in a dingy rowing out to the boat. He had insisted on rowing which was a challenge and comical. The needed coordination to manage two oars simultaneously and in rhythm as one propels a boat in a desired direction is a little harder than it appears. For those of us who have been rowing boats since we were old enough to hold the oars, no problem—but for a thirty-six year old man who had no experience or instruction—always good for a few laughs! I really expected to end up swimming to the boat but, much to my surprise, we made it aboard, dry.

Off came the canvas hood and into the boat we climbed. Father Matt was so excited. He'd never been on a boat that had a galley and, in a condensed version, all the comforts of home. Once he'd checked the ups, downs and all-a-rounds of the vessel I started the engine. I raised anchor and we began to steam out of the harbor. There were many yachts moored and attention to proximity was essential. Boats shift very quickly with tidal activity and could result in an immediate change of direction hence, maneuvering to open water required undivided attention. For Father Matt, focusing for a long period of time was a bit of a demand. As long as he wasn't at the helm, we were fine.

The day could not have been more beautiful. The sun was shining, temperature hovering in the mid-eighties, little to no breeze and ideal water conditions. Destination: Cook's Corner Restaurant. The trip was a thirty-five to forty minute ride. Since lunch was the purpose of our mini cruise, we had a couple of extra hours to relax, explore and savor each moment. Navigating the adventure was easy because there was no need to put out to sea. Simply following the coastline would eventually get us to our target. As an added benefit, it would also give Father Matt a chance to see the beauty of the rocky coast of Maine up close and personal. The luxury of time afforded us a great opportunity to tuck into a cove or two, drop anchor and jump into the refreshing, crystal clear water.

I was the first to jump in. Although the temperature of cove water tended to be a little warmer than in the harbor, it was still invigorating. After much encouragement, Father Matt gave in and made the plunge. He quickly popped up from being underwater and let out a shriek! Unaccustomed to salt water swimming, the experience for him was slightly different than that of diving into a heated pool! He quickly became acclimated to his new milieu and began playing as he chased and splashed about. It had been years since I had played cat and mouse games; perhaps even so far back as when I was a teenager. What fun it was to return to those care-free times!

Following what seemed like hours in the water, we made our way to the shore, stretched out on a tiny pebble-covered beach and basked in the sun for a bit. Soon, the incoming tide had reached us; as each wave gently rolled in, reaching higher and higher, the water tickled our toes and made us both laugh. That was our cue that time was moving on and so should we.

"It's that time," I said. As I moved toward the water, I quickly glanced over my shoulder to see if Father Matt was following. He hadn't moved and seemed reluctant to do that.

"Come on, chicken, last one to the boat drives!" I said to him. What a set-up. Needless to say he didn't rush to beat me, but it did inspire him to stir. I waited for him to reach the boat as we both climbed onto the diver's platform that extended from the stern of the vessel. Once aboard, we both dried off, lifted anchor and were off.

Merrily on our way, we weaved in and out of several of the many indentions that are carved along the shoreline. Although unspoken, the anxiety of taking the helm was clearly written on Father Matt's face. The time had come to make a sailor out of this priest, so I did.

He steamed along well-controlled, focused and respectful of the sea. The huge smile on his face was a clear display that he just loved being captain. Turning toward me for approval, I nodded and he carefully veered the boat into a cove. He was taken by the beauty that surrounded him and was distracted. I spotted a sandbar that was a safe distance from us. Since he hadn't yet seen it and once he did, probably wouldn't properly calculate the distance between it and the boat, I called him to task.

"Sandbar," I called out, knowing that we had plenty of room. Father Matt reacted immediately and calmly. He did very well. He remembered the routine and executed the steps properly. No disaster was hatched and a lesson was well learned. I never told him my little secret of plenty of room between us and the sandbar and he never asked. From that moment on he felt like a hero and that was okay.

Perfect

As we approached Cook's, I took over the helm. We entered the heavily populated cove bordered by the peninsula on one side and the mainland on the other. As I negotiated the vessel into the available slip, Father Matt hopped out onto the wharf, bowline in tow, and tied up. Once the stern was also safely secured, we both headed up the ramp and into the restaurant.

The place was overflowing with customers. The beautiful day combined with the restaurant's reputation and location was appealing to many. The eatery was situated just above the rocks overlooking the water. Boats of all sizes and shapes were moored, tied up or just floating in the water. Gulls with expanded wings lurked overhead waiting to alter their flying pattern that would bring them down to scoop up any food that was discarded. The smell of the salt water permeated every breath and the air was filled with the bouquet of cooked shellfish and blueberry cake. Waiting was difficult but worth it.

"Number three, three, three," echoed from the outdoor sound system.

"Yes! That's us," said Father Matt. We ran up the rocks from where we had been sitting for the past forty-five minutes. Once in the restaurant, we were led to our table.

"Long wait but you'll love every bite," I said to Father Matt.

"I'm sure, but you know what? The smell is making me crazy! I need to reward myself for this long, excruciating wait so I'm going with a full-blown shore dinner. What about you?"

"Indeed, sounds like a plan to me," I responded. "I'll have mussels as opposed to steamers, though. There's one thing that you can be certain about if you order lobster here. You know that these crustaceans slept in Casco Bay last night. It just doesn't get much fresher than that!"

"Nor does it get much better than this," was Father Matt's comment, "Not much better than this…"

Enhanced by cold Perrier, lunch was perfect—and so was this first day of sailing together.

CHAPTER 11

F ourth of July—the name changed from Father Matt to Matthew. Father Matt arrived at the cottage mid morning that day. For a change, this was not a spontaneous visit; both of us had actually collaborated on planning this holiday. Prior to his arrival, I had rowed out and brought the boat back to the wharf. Lunch and dinner were onboard, gas tank was full, and the ground tackle had been checked and was tight. She was ready. Within minutes of his arrival, we had boarded and were underway, heading out to Portland Harbor to watch the evening's fireworks.

The ocean was absolutely beautiful! The sea sparkled from the sun, the friendly porpoises gracefully weaved in and out of the water, an occasional seal popped up to satisfy his curious nature and at full power we glided ever so gracefully through the waves.

What a wonderful opportunity to enjoy nature's most beautiful gifts, was my thought. Simultaneously, Father Matt spoke up, "How about we stop the engine and just drift for a while, Kate? Can we do that? We could just enjoy this beauty and maybe a little later have lunch."

"Sounds perfect to me," I replied. Within seconds, the vastness of the open sea carried the sound of silence. The vessel began to drift slowly, smoothly and ever so quietly, much like our relationship. We made our way to the bow of the boat and stretched out along the deck. How calming—just us and the sea. The only sound to hear was that of water splashing as our porpoise friends reentered their domain following their graceful leaps through the air. Their antics were whimsical and flowed with such rhythm that hearing them was soothing. I felt so relaxed that I closed my eyes and just drifted in cadence with the flow of the boat. I came out of my trance in what I thought to be moments later but in fact found it was well over thirty minutes. My growling stomach combined with the position of the sun in the sky indicated that time had really flown by, and it was probably just about high noon. As I looked around, Father Matt was nowhere to be seen but I could hear him rustling around in the cabin.

Holding onto the grab rails, I carefully made my way along the starboard of the boat. As I stepped down onto the floorboard, Father Matt appeared. He'd been down in the galley preparing lunch. He was carrying a tray of crackers and cheeses with wine glasses filled with sparkling water. We climbed over the stern and set up our little impromptu dining area on the diver's platform. Once situated, we dangled our feet in nature's very own spa. We enjoyed good food, good company and the golden sound of silence. Dessert consisted of basking in the sun, lavishing in the comfort of receiving a wonderful salt water foot massage, being entertained by the porpoises that had followed the boat for miles and thoroughly enjoying being in harmony with all the beauty that Mother Nature had to offer.

As much as I wanted to spend eternity in that precise spot doing exactly what we had been doing, the position of the sun in the sky alerted me that it was time to go. Still quite a distance away from our destination, Father Matt took care of the food detail and I started up the engine. Soon we were underway, en route to the evening's celebration.

We pulled into port shortly after the hour had passed and many vessels had already arrived. For the most part, yachting families are very courteous and conscientious of their surroundings. Although formal arrangements as to boat placement were not part of the plan, an unwritten and unspoken but very much respected law governed group behavior at gatherings of this size. Hundreds of boats quietly milled around the bay with all of us having spontaneously dropped into rank by order of arrival. As we followed in cadence, the power boats and sailboats combined to produce a display of beautiful colors, shapes and sizes. The lead boat was the harbor master and, at the appropriate time, he signaled to drop anchor and thus each boat's chosen spot for the evening had been determined.

Perfect

Boats that had come in multiples had their own area in which they formed a sort of "wagon circle" whereby friends tied up to friends making one another's home on the sea accessible. We were an independent vessel and moored some distance from any other boat. In preparation for the fireworks, we made ourselves comfortable on reclining chairs out on the floorboards of the stern with a table of munchies and sparkling water between us. A bit early just yet, we simply relaxed and enjoyed the comforts that can only be experienced on the sea.

Only too soon it was curtain time! Nature's lights had dimmed and the skies were lit up with streams of bright, beautiful colors that created handsome formations. The banging, crackling and whistling as those firecrackers blazed their way into the heavens added so much excitement to the event. These magnificent displays of patriotism went on for one and a half hours.

The celebration was a perfect fit. Father Matt and I enjoyed every moment even though little dialogue was exchanged. There was no need for words, our expressions said it all. The finale was spectacular. Simultaneously, and so very excited, Father Matt and I spontaneously jumped to our feet. Behold! A stage, decorated in lights that spelled U.S.A. had been erected on a float in the center of the harbor. On it stood a local radio show host as announcer along with several dozen members of a local community choir. Their angelic voices rang throughout the universe as they sang our national anthem. The very last firecrackers were released as Old Glory spread across the sky with red, white and blue bombs bursting on both sides. I could feel the chills going up and down my spine as I nearly exploded with pride. Father Matt was feeling the same emotional high and in the midst of it all, his arms had found their way around my waist. As his embrace tightened, I leaned against him. The evening celebration had ended; ours had just begun. I turned toward the bow of the boat as I felt both of his arms holding me back. His gesture was so gentle that as I took that first step, I walked right out of his embrace.

I didn't want to walk away. I wanted so much to stay. I turned in attempt to recover and immediately found myself totally en-

47

gulfed in Matthew's arms once again. Although many boats were still moored, it was as though we were totally alone under this magnificent starlit night. As a slight breeze enveloped us, his caress felt secure—so reassuring, so comforting, so loving. I felt this was exactly where I belonged.

Matthew's hands gently followed the contour of my face as he softly kissed my forehead, eyes, tip of my nose and finally, my mouth. Then the inevitable followed. That precious moment of the first kiss is like no other. This intimacy felt so right, but how truthful was it for a kiss to be shared between a woman and a priest?

CHAPTER 12

Suddenly my relaxing and very enjoyable visit into the past was interrupted as the car swerved off to the side of the road. That abrupt, angular action taken to avoid being sideswiped jolted me back to reality—the same cold, silent truth that I had escaped from some time ago still permeated the air. Once again, I looked over at Matthew. Still, there was nothing. Not even an apology for the sudden, totally unexpected deviation of the vehicle's direction. His expression was blank; he had what almost appeared to be a mean configuration to an otherwise very handsome face. Had he suddenly become a psychopath? Was this bi-polar like behavior triggered by sweet wine having gone sour? Not afraid of him, but skeptical, I was hoping that we would soon be home.

Finding myself in the middle of a situation that totally confused me, I asked myself: Where is the man that I love? What has happened to him?

My answer: He's gone—absolutely gone. This gentle man, the man who said over and over again that he loved me with all of his heart was behind that wheel once upon a time, but not now. He was not only my friend, he was my confidant, my lover, my soul mate and most important, he was the father of my baby. And now—he'd disappeared. It was almost like a Jekyll and Hyde scenario and equally as disconcerting.

Somehow, this very same person had been transformed. This man who today was willing to take his own baby's life must view himself as a supreme authority over all souls.

Tomorrow, this very same person, this Roman Catholic priest will sit in a confessional and pardon the sins that he hears from parishioners coming for forgiveness; he will give these alleged sinners penance and send them on their way. He will celebrate mass before a congregation who view him as God's representative here on earth. He will take Holy Communion and then give it to all those who will receive. He will do all of this—following the foiled plan of having traveled to New York to have the life of his child terminated. The man that I had fallen in love with was not this creature.

I was rehashing all of these thoughts, to a point where they were coming at me so rapidly and furiously that I gasped aloud. A slight turn of Matthew's head indicated that he had heard me, but he maintained his steadfast silence and never inquired as to whether or not I was all right or might have some need.

Very angry with me and certainly more concerned about himself than about his child's well-being or mine, Matthew continued to drive in silence. This man, who was so caring and affectionate toward me twenty-four hours ago, never asked how I felt, if I was hungry (I hadn't eaten since the evening before) or if I was experiencing any discomforts. In his eyes, he had been betrayed. That certainly wasn't settling well. Matthew's focus at this time reverted back to himself, and only himself. Nothing and no one else mattered. Maybe this perfect man wasn't so perfect at all.

These thoughts were making me sick to my stomach, and in self defense I needed to take myself back to the world as I wanted to remember it.

CHAPTER 13

I closed my eyes and allowed myself to drift back to happy times. It was July 1970. The relationship that I shared with Matthew had taken on a whole new dimension. He had become not only my friend and my soul mate but also my lover.

It had been a beautiful afternoon. Matthew and I had been out on the boat and had tucked it in one of the coves where we swam, played in the refreshing water and cooked dinner over a fire on the rocks beside the inlet's edge. Shortly after we had returned to the cottage, a fog bank rolled in. With the fog came dampness. So for the first time that summer, we lit a fire in the Franklin fireplace. The flickering flames and soft lights created an ambience that encouraged our enjoying one another's company as we cuddled on the white bear rug that stretched across the middle of the living room floor. That white bear rug became the bed of sweet surrender.

I didn't want those flames to die. I forever wanted to stay in the moment of fitting so perfectly into Matthew's arms. It felt so right. I started to wonder about the inappropriateness of our relationship as tears began to fall to my cheeks. Although I didn't make a sound, a tear or two must have crossed onto Matthew's chest because he pulled away, placed his hand on my cheek and softly asked why I was crying. Somewhat embarrassed and not certain of what to say, I just nestled back into the curve of his body.

"Does it bother you that I'm a priest, Kate?"

"I think so," was my response, "It feels so right, so why should it be wrong?"

"It's not, Kate. It's not. I was born a man long before I became a priest, my darling, so, to be true to my very primitive being is to be true to my beginning and to pursue my love for you, Kate," he said with much conviction.

His love for me—we had never spoken the word love before. And to pursue his love for me—what exactly did that mean? I needed to know and so I asked.

"I love you, Kate, and I don't want life without you. Everything is too new right now to determine how to work this out. Just have faith in me, and in time, I'll handle it when it's right. Do you love me enough to do that?"

Did I love him enough to wait? Could I believe that the white collar was but a marking of deception? Was I convinced that someday soon, we would be together forever in the real world? Could Matt leave the priesthood and all its securities? I quickly answered these questions for myself. Yes, yes, yes and yes. Since the numbers added up, I embarked upon this journey trespassing onto forbidden land and trusted that I was making the right decision. Because he loves me, he won't hurt me. So--- here goes!

"Yes!" I responded ever so much louder than I had expected, "Yes!"

Matthew took me into his arms and once again we sealed our love for one another. Blended as one, the immoral pleasure of indulgence was just so perfect.

From that point many of our discussions were animated. Our quiet times, heart-to-heart talk times were mostly late at night as we watched a fire, walked between rain drops or gazed at a sparkling sky. With every day our love grew deeper and deeper. My heart knew that this was a no-win situation for both of us, no matter what Matthew would say. We would occasionally discuss the collision course that we were on, but it never seemed to change anything. We were both willing to continue our journey blindfolded. Matthew had plotted the course; he was navigating our journey and it was paradise. I was very content and truly believed that together, we could weather any storm. I had surrendered all control and was ready to cast off. Onward, Captain!

Matthew took up regular residence at the cottage. He would commute from Blackstone to his parish, go about his daily business and then come home to me at the end of the day. If he had an early mass to say the following morning, he would stay the night in the rectory. We were spending many hours together and life was at its best. As for company and neighbors, everyone knew him as Matt, no one being the wiser that he was a priest, including my aunt and uncle who had their home three cottages from where I was located. We were on a real adventure and did everything from spending overnights out on the water to installing a new carpet in the living room of the cottage. Since Matthew had never before gotten his hands dirty from doing manual labor, the carpet ordeal in the dead heat of summer was certainly an experience that he probably would not want to repeat.

The summer progressed and Matthew took a week's vacation. We were off to Canada, taking our time dropping in and out of little villages along the way. We stayed in cozy, little cabins that we found on route and attended French soirees in an attempt to experience the real Canadian flavor of life. We enjoyed a Friday night dance with a touch of folklore, a Saturday night community dinner and a Sunday afternoon *concert de canton*. These experiences were so enriching. Not knowing anyone was ideal for us. Although we were total strangers, our eagerness to drink up the natural ambience of the environment was very impressive to the village people. They welcomed us into their families with warmth and sincerity.

It really wasn't essential that Matthew travel incognito, feeling quite safe that we were far enough away from home not to run into anyone who would recognize him. On one particular day we boarded a ferry to cross the St. Lawrence into Quebec. We made our way to the portside railing of the barge-sized vessel and planned to remain there for the crossing.

Totally enthralled in watching the gulls as they flew into the boat's backdraft that allowed them to rest as the air current carried their streamlined bodies, Matthew never noticed a woman who was slowly making her way through the crowd and heading in our direction. He turned and happened to spot her just moments before she reached him. She was one of his parishioners, and obviously recognized him. Without skipping a beat, he immediately leaned toward me with instructions as to how to react as she approached. Midway, he felt a tap on his shoulder.

"Father Matt." said the voice, "Father Matt."

He very nonchalantly turned toward this lady saying, "Excuse me?"

"Father Matt, you know me," she said so very excited probably about unexpectedly meeting her parish priest so far away from home. I don't think that she had put me in the same picture frame at that point.

"I'm very sorry, Madame," he said with such conviction, "but I'm afraid that you're mistaken. I assure you, I am not your priest—my wife and I are traveling to Quebec City from our home in Massachusetts. But, I must say, you mistaking me for your priest is quite a compliment to him. Enjoy your trip!"

"Oh my, I am sorry. You are his twin. Everybody has a twin they say, and you are certainly his. I'm sorry to have disturbed you. I can't wait to tell Father Matt that I met his twin."

"I'm sure he'll be happy to hear that, good day." And Matthew turned toward me, put his arm around my waist and sighed ever so deeply. I, on the other hand, thought that my legs would crumble beneath me. Successful at convincing someone that you are not who you really are—that was Matthew. He had done it again. Was he that insincere or was he just a good actor, able to pull off pretty much anything that he would put his mind to? Scary thoughts that I certainly didn't want to entertain, so I quickly erased them from my mind, not expecting that they would ever return to haunt me.

Upon reaching the shores of Quebec City, we disembarked. I was never so happy to touch land! If anyone looks familiar, we'll run, I thought. No more impromptu performances.

Matthew and I checked into le Chateau Frontenac, and as we followed the bellhop to our room I was totally overwhelmed by the beauty of this castle. I was hungry and anxious to visit the Old City of Quebec with its cobblestone streets and artists. There was a small area that resembled Montmartre in Paris. In France, this is a quaint cobblestone courtyard behind Notre Dame Cathedral that has outdoor cafés on one side and artists and their work on the other. In Quebec, both cafés and artists were on a long, narrow street in the lower city.

Artists displayed their wares and painted and drew caricatures while the patron waited. I was totally in awe from the aura that wrapped around me. I really enjoyed the aroma and taste of freshly brewed gourmet coffee and hot breads just out of the ovens that these tiny sidewalk shops served. I gathered such pleasure from watching the artists start with a blank canvas and magically turn it into a colorful masterpiece of their interpretation. The uniqueness of what lies in the eyes of the beholder would never be duplicated. Matthew was equally attracted to the arts.

I was also a people watcher. I loved and respected the opportunity to watch people, in a nice way, especially in a small concentrated area that was heavily traveled by tourists. I saw such symbolism in that experience. Hundreds of thousands of people from all over the world would assemble within a small radius, melding their cultures, sitting at tables beside one another, nodding a greeting to strangers, and while speaking many different languages, harmonizing the sounds of their voices into one beautiful melody. Just for those few moments, people from all over the world, from many different nations, were at peace. "Why can't the brotherhood that tourists share become the way of life throughout the world?" I asked Matthew.

"You're so global, Kate; who ever would ask that question except you. It's unfortunate that more people don't think that way."

Matthew took advantage of this down time with me. We were sitting at a sidewalk café sipping gourmet French Roast coffee and basking in the artistic delights. He reached over the table, cupped my hand between his and stared into my dark brown eyes.

"The eyes are the windows to your soul, the saying goes, and I can see what you're feeling right this minute, Kate. You radiate a love that seems to envelop me in a state in which I am floating on a soft, puffy white cloud—a totally free spirit—liberated to love the woman that I have longed for all of my life," he said.

"Yikes! A little frightening," I thought, but not wanting him to stop.

"Kate, what is it about you that attracts me so?"

I raised my eyebrows and smiled. I bit my lower lip very gently, a habit that I had when I was embarrassed or stuck for words.

J. C. Soucier

In the less happy times, I attempted to prevent myself from crying by doing the same thing. This definitely was a reaction to being embarrassed.

"Let's see, you're energetic, attractive and you're petite enough for me to scoop up if I want. Your frosted blond hair frames your very dark brown eyes and your gentle face is carefree and truly reflects your style. What do you think? Are those the reasons why I love you? Or, could it be because you're a lady who is well-mannered and soft-spoken. You have a *joie de vivre* that is infectious; you're light yet intense, you're intelligent, educated, well-traveled and you know and love many of the arts. Is that why I love you? No, none or all of the above, but most of all, Kate, I love you because you're you!"

He's gone wild, I thought, it must be the Canadian air! Even though I was thoroughly enjoying the many compliments coming my way from a very biased Matthew, I had heard enough. I squeezed his hand, winked at him and slowly rose from my chair pulling him up behind me.

"Let's walk around and see what these talented people have to show us," I said. Without reservation, Matthew clutched my hand tightly and willingly followed.

We sauntered up and down the narrow, cobblestone alley enjoying the many beautiful works of art that were displayed as well as masterpieces in progress. I saw one particular watercolor that I very much liked, but decided to forgo an immediate purchase. We continued our tour for nearly two more hours.

Time was not of the essence, when to eat was not dictated by any certain schedule. There were, however, enticing factors in it all. There was the smell of freshly baked bread followed by the aroma of newly brewed coffee complemented by the delightful opportunity to simply sit, watch the world go by and indulge in foods that were unique to this little piece of Quebec City. The time to stop had become evident to us both; without a beat, Matthew said, "How about we stop here for a bite to eat, Kate?"

"Terrific idea, Matthew, I'm ready."

Within moments, the maitre d' seated us. No sooner had we settled in, a young, seasoned waiter was at our side, menus in hand

and ready to serve us the beverage of our choice.

"*Une mocha latte, s'il vous plait,*" I said.

Matthew immediately followed by adding, "*Moi aussi— merci.*" As we waited for our mocha latte to be delivered we browsed the menu.

"How about we splurge and have crepes with chocolate ice cream, maple syrup topped with raspberries and whipped cream?"

"Feeling kittenish and impish, I said: "Oh my heaven, how much sweeter can it get? Okay Matthew, let's do it!

"Please order for me, Kate and I'll be right back." Without any further explanation, Matthew rose from the table and walked away. Although I saw him heading out of the café, I never gave his direction or destination a second thought.

Sitting in my own little world, I floated away into a daydream as I gazed out into the alleyway. I thought of how very much I loved Matthew—and how wonderful it was to be in such a romantic city with him. Everything seemed so perfect, even the uneven cobblestones that marked the path of the artists' alley were a perfect fit to the picture.

The word, Mademoiselle spoken by the waiter startled me a bit and quickly brought me back to reality. He had returned and was ready to record my culinary wish. With a grin on my face and a sparkle in my eye, I placed a double order of what had to be the most mouth-watering attraction on the menu.

Glowing with pride to have placed an order that was so adventurous, I straightened myself in the chair and smiled. Feeling extremely pompous and exuding excitement, I couldn't wait to tell Matthew the "mission had been accomplished" and that he'd best be ready for the treat.

The mocha lattes had been served and I was sipping on mine. Suddenly, poof! Like a genie, Matthew appeared with a large package under his right arm. He walked over to me, leaned forward and kissed me tenderly on the forehead.

"I love you, Kate," he whispered, as he presented me with the parcel wrapped in white paper that was held closed with a string secured by a knot and bow. Completely taken off guard, I moved my latte and placed the package partially on the table. I carefully

J. C. Soucier

dislodged the string and removed the paper. Once unwrapped, there lay the beautiful watercolor I so admired.

"I love it, Matthew—almost as much as I love you," I said in a playful yet very appreciative voice. This work reflected the very place in Quebec where we were that actual moment. The cobblestone alley, café and boutiques had been captured by the artist and, oddly enough, the focal point of the picture was the café where we were about to have an unforgettable eating experience. Everything about the day was in that picture including the soft colors that described the gentleness of our love.

Our week together in Quebec went much too quickly. The morning to head back arrived. With that came the reality of the nature of our relationship. Would we ever be together publicly and as free as we had been that past week? No is the very truthful, correct answer to this question, no matter how much I want to believe differently. As I was walking toward the car, tears fell to the ground, releasing the feelings that words couldn't express.

CHAPTER 14

August sun—August moon—August stars—August rain—all wonderful venues for a romance that I hoped would never end. As the days passed, the intensity of our relationship grew deeper and deeper.

My memories had taken me back to August of 1970. Vivid as though it had been today, I remembered them so well. How perfect we were together. We would awake to see the sunrise, hear the birds, beat the squirrels to their feeding ground and swim in the early morning sun.

"How can anyone not see how very much in love we are, Kate?" Matthew would say every now and then. "My eyes must tell the world!" His sparkling ocean blue eyes were indeed very much alive, more so than they had been ever before. When we exchanged glances the message had to have been written in neon lights! There was no question that we were very much in love, but for now, it would continue to remain our secret. To date, Matthew had been very successful at keeping his two lives totally disassociated; to make a choice at this time would be premature. He was comfortable juggling two different worlds.

Having two separate worlds didn't seem to affect the beauty of our being together. The danger got lost in the shuffle. Although day after day new experiences fed into the intriguing aura that enveloped our love, I would occasionally find a moment when skepticism would sneak in. Can anything this beautiful last? I would ask myself. Why haven't I heard others speak of feeling such ecstasy in the relationship that they share? What do we have that no one else seems to have? Is there something magical about Matthew and me? Or, could it be that the forbidden fruit is ever so much sweeter? I never allowed myself to look any further for answers.

J. C. Soucier

It was another beautiful Friday morning. Matthew had left about 6:30 a.m. I had followed my morning ritual and was sitting on the porch drinking coffee and enjoying the peacefulness and nature's beauty. About 11:30 a.m. the phone rang. I bounced up to answer it. It was Matthew. That call was very much out of the ordinary; although I was excited to hear from him, I just could not imagine why he called. What was so important that it couldn't wait until he returned later that afternoon?

"Kate," he said, "you need to come to the rectory as soon as possible."

"Excuse me?"

"You need to come to the rectory as soon as possible."

"Why? Can't whatever it is wait until you come home?"

"No…I…just come now."

"Will you tell me what this is all about? Why so urgent?"

"No, just trust me, Kate. Come to the office section of the building and enter through the front door. I'll be looking for you. Will you come right along?"

"Yes, I'll come as quickly as I can get there."

The whole conversation was intimidating to me. I knew that something terribly wrong had happened, but I had absolutely no idea what it could be. Thoroughly confused, I changed from my play clothes to more professional attire. I ran to my car, started the engine and was off. On route to the city, I tried and tried to figure out what this mysterious and very frightening call was all about. It was so out of character for Matthew to be that formal with me. He sounded as though he was reading from a script. And evasive—he totally refused to give me any idea of what this was about. Although he was a prankster and a lover of intrigue, to be this secretive and official with me was totally unrecognizable as Matthew's style. Something very, very bad had to have happened, but what?

I pulled into the rectory parking lot and just sat there for a moment. I was so frightened, I was sick to my stomach. I opened the door to my car and stepped out. As I slowly walked toward the office door I saw Matthew waiting there for me.

He opened the door and I entered. No greeting, no hug. He turned on his heels and walked into his office. I followed. Although I had been in the rectory before, I'd never been in this particular office. The room was desolate, empty with nothing but a bookcase barren of books and a picture of Pope Paul VI on one wall and that of the bishop on the other. His desk was bare, lovely but bare. There was a telephone, what appeared to be an appointment book, a pad of paper and a pen sitting on a shiny mahogany surface. The office was sterile, just plain sterile. I could see how a priest in his commanding black suit could easily dominate anyone who may be sitting across from him. This particular morning was no different.

Matthew began to speak—in a chilled, formal voice.

"I've just returned from the bishop's office, Kate. It appears that Bob has been busy. Apparently, he followed me to your cottage yesterday. Why? I don't know except I do know that he went directly from Blackstone to the Chancery. Although he didn't have an appointment, he demanded to see the bishop. Unusual as it may be, the bishop left a meeting already in session and accommodated Bob. It was then that he announced to his Excellency that you and I were having a love affair. My understanding is that without much further conversation, the bishop dismissed him. When I arrived this morning there was a message in my box that I was to meet with his Excellency at 9 a.m. today."

I had nowhere to go. I had nothing to say. I simply sank into my chair as tears began rolling down my cheeks. As I looked up, the sparkle in Matthew's eyes was gone, there was no smile and his voice was unfamiliar.

"This is it, Kate, we can't see each other again. This has to end as of this moment. I'll need to retrieve my things from the cottage; perhaps it would be best if we made plans for me to go at a time when you will not be there. No need to make it any harder than it is for either of us."

His heart had been broken. My heart had been yanked from my chest. His demeanor weakened and with what appeared to be his last ounce of courage, he softly said, "Kate, I love you and I will always love you. Our life together has been the best thing that has ever happened to me, but I can't leave the priesthood and go out into such a wild world totally unprepared. How would I support you? Where would I get employment? As an ex-priest I would probably be treated as an outcast and that would reflect on you as well. I want the very best for you and, as a lay person I couldn't give that to you. We'll have to settle for knowing that we share this love that is so very intense—and it is exclusively ours forever. I so wish there was another way, Kate. I am so sorry to hurt you."

Still sitting limp in the chair, I just wanted to die. My whole life had been taken away from me. I didn't want life without Matthew; what would I do? My tears began to flow uncontrollably. This man who had professed his love for me just hours before, suddenly was no longer a part of my life. In this split moment, he was gone—everything was gone. It was over.

"Kate, please say something—I don't want to do this... please..."

Feeling totally numb and just unable to respond, I slowly rose from my chair, turned and walked toward the door. I stopped momentarily, looked back at Matthew and softly whispered, "I love you," and then continued to walk out of the office and to my car. Matthew was standing, but never made a move to follow me to the door. I could feel him being torn---as his eyes watched my every move. I opened the door and slid into my car. I didn't fall apart quite then in fear that someone might have been looking out a window or walking by and would take notice. There was but one place that I wanted to be right now, and that was sitting in the rocking chair on the porch at my cottage. I headed home.

CHAPTER 15

A s I drove the distance, I sobbed all the way. At times, I was crying so hysterically that I had to pull over to the side of the road.

"I must get home," I said sobbing, "I must get home." Not a minute too soon, I drove into my driveway at Blackstone. I turned off the engine and just sat there, totally lifeless, too limp to move. I really wanted to get to my security blanket, but climbing the stairs to the rocking chair on the porch seemed like an insurmountable task, so I didn't leave the car.

He's gone, gone…,forever, Matthew is gone. And I cried.

How could my own relative do this? He was also Matthew's very good friend—why? This is the same person who was responsible for initiating everything; he planned all the parties and he invited me to join them. Whatever motivated him to pry into someone else's business? Why would anyone go to the extreme that Bob did? What is the driving force to destroy us? Does Jeanne know this? She's my very best friend—why wouldn't she have warned me? I just don't understand. All these questions were racing around in my head and no answers to any of them. I had no answers—no answers.

Completed exhausted, I fell asleep. When I awoke, my emotions were like those of a wild animal that had just been captured. I wanted to attack. I wanted to hurt the man who had robbed me of tomorrow. In my eyes, at that moment, my future was in total shambles with no recourse as to how to put all the pieces back together again. I started to sob and scream.

What seemed like hours later, I felt somewhat more calm and in control. It was then that I realized that I was totally drenched with tears. My blouse was wet, my hair was dripping, my slacks stuck to my legs and I didn't even care. I was so hurt, how I felt physically just didn't matter.

I converted to being very quiet as I got out of the car and headed toward the porch. Looking up, I imagined that I could see the swing that was hung from the porch so many years ago, and I could envision my dad sitting on the rocking chair watching me enjoy the security and comfort of being with him.

"Daddy, Daddy, I need you so," I cried. He didn't answer. Twenty years had lapsed. I had grown up and my dad was at home recuperating from a heart attack. I didn't think that he knew anything about Matthew—but he did. Thinking back to a recent conversation that we had shared, I realized that he had smoothly slid in a bit of advice that I never recognized until that very moment.

"Make sure, Baby, that when you give your heart away, you give it to someone who is free to accept it," were his words.

Oh Daddy, you knew didn't you—you knew. He always knew everything. I remember well the day I skipped school for the very first time, three weeks before graduation. I was a high school senior and the day was a beautiful, warm spring day. All my friends were going swimming instead of school. I followed. I got home that day at the regular time as though I had been to school, and my dad was sitting at the kitchen table sipping coffee. It was mid-afternoon. He should have been at work, but he was at home—because he knew.

I thought, "Can I keep this away from him? He will call just to say hello and tell me that he loves me as he did every day. What will I say to him? Should I tell him? I can't lie. He would pick that up in a second. I can't burden him with my heartache. My hurt will be his hurt; he's too sick to handle this. He needs not to worry. His recovery requires believing that his daughter is doing just fine. And he will believe just that."

As I finally reached the top of the stairs, I glanced over at the rocking chair that Matthew would normally sit in. Since I had left in such a hurry, the dishes had not been picked up, so his coffee cup of the morning was still on the table. I bit my lip in attempt to stop the tears. Gingerly I sat in his chair. I ran my hands up and down the wood where his arms had rested, wanting so much to feel him there. I turned toward the table and reached over, took his cup and caressed it. My finger followed the circle around the rim that had touched his lips. All that was left was a memory. I held the bright orange porcelain mug ever so closely—and cried.

"I'm just fine, Daddy," I whispered softly as the tears streamed down my face and onto my hands that held the cold coffee cup. "I'm just fine."

CHAPTER 16

The cottage was cold and lonely—not a fun place to be anymore. At the beginning, I couldn't face anyone. I spoke to my dad over the phone and that took every ounce of energy that I had—because I truly needed for him to believe that I was just fine. Many of my friends who visited me throughout the summer would also stop in to see my dad as he was convalescing at home. I knew that it was but a matter of time before someone would mention my inactivity and inability to be available for their escapades out onto the deep blue sea. So, I needed a plan, a plan that would help me conceal the reason why my lifestyle had taken such a dramatic turn.

At first, even being near the ocean was very difficult for me. Everything, just everything was overloaded with memories of Matthew. The cottage, the porch, his footprints in the grass, the dock, the rocks, the boats—it was all him. Now, I was so alone. I was missing what had become half of my everyday life, the half that was needed to complete the perfect circle of love.

As an escape, I would walk down to the shore, find a niche in a rock and just tuck myself into it. I brought along some books to read, knowing that I could solicit comfort from them. Occasionally, I would find sentences, quotes, anecdotes, phrases, sonnets that seemed so related, appropriate. One of those was written by Roselle Mercier Montgomery in *The Stowaway*:

"Never a ship sails out of the bay,
But carries my heart as a stowaway—"

Needless to say, I pondered upon those words for a long time.

Nearly a week had passed since that fateful day, and I had spent most of my time sitting down by the water, reading and crying. I had unplugged my phone. I called my dad but that was my only outside contact. I didn't put up the white towel for Lois to visit. I refused to respond to the telephone calls and messages that were being delivered by my kind neighbor. Although Matthew was relentless in trying to connect with me, his attempts were to no avail. He never had quite enough courage to personally make an appearance.

I wanted to be alone. I wanted the privilege of being unaccompanied as I navigated the course through the turbulent waters of this journey. I needed to try to make sense out of what had happened. Eventually, it would all add up, but when? Having the luxury of being totally uninterrupted, my mind began to review, then filter, screen, identify and ultimately solve the problem.

Bob was married to Jeanne. He was a relative by marriage only. He also appeared to be a good friend of Matthew's. A popular, very active guy, he was the president of the parish council, a member of the Diocesan Human Relations Services Board of Directors, which was the social service agency of the Catholic Church, and served on a number of other community-related committees. Viewed as a pillar of his Church, Bob was a model parishioner, seen as a good family man, strong in his faith and a wonderful and loving husband and father.

He was always in the center of organizing most of the social activities that brought his group of friends together, including Matthew and me. He was the host that would do it all—what a hero!

The more I thought about Bob, the person he appeared to be and the person that had recently broken out of his cocoon, the more often the word "narcissistic" popped into my mind. I became annoyed with not being able to go beyond this personality disorder that attached itself to Bob's name. It was a hunch, but I just couldn't get it out of my mind. Exasperated, I spontaneously ran up to the cottage, changed my clothes, jumped into my car and headed for the college library. Once there, I literally ran into the building. I just couldn't wait to focus in on this gut feeling that was gnawing away at me. I located the resource books that I needed and settled down to begin my research.

As I read and read, I seemed to find more and more to jot down; keywords that later would hopefully give me a short but full description of a narcissistic personality disorder. I tore off the scratch paper from the pad that I'd been scribbling on and began to draw a more organized two-column table. The first column would be dedicated to behavioral terminology and the other as to how it applied to Bob. Once completed, it would hopefully help me to see a clearer picture, thereby enabling me to begin to fit pieces of this crazy puzzle together. Ultimately, I hoped that I could understand.

Bingo! These words fell right into place and became a complete description of Bob's behavior and lifestyle. Being ever so far away from knowing anything about a person's psychological makeup, I would never have dared to label him, except to myself. A person who can totally destroy his relative and his best friend has to be somehow frighteningly disturbed. This side of him was very scary and dangerous. Suddenly a thought crossed my mind. Had this obsession started way back when I was in Paris and found a post card of Omar Sharif? The one that I had sent to Matthew in care of Bob and Jeanne's address? The very one that Matthew never received? Could this have been the beginning of this insane behavior? Had Bob been stalking our every move from that point on? If so, his mission had been accomplished. He had successfully robbed us of any possible future that we had together.

The pillar was beginning to crumble. Bob's very own surreptitious, sneaky lifestyle was closing in on him; however, his lack of conscience and need to continue living in his fantasy world meant that he would use any and all measures to protect himself—no matter at whose expense. He was desperate. He needed to find a smokescreen that would expose someone other than himself and his own shortcomings. So Bob discovered a mysterious relationship that, if it surfaced, had flares that would be bright enough to blind everyone, hence allowing him to hide his little covert operation. He was right—it did.

In my mind, who, why and when had been answered. I left the library feeling somewhat more liberated. The weight that I had carried around for nearly two weeks seemed to have been lifted. Now that I had some answers, I would be able to stabilize myself and move on.

Returning to the peace and solitude that the grand Atlantic

J. C. Soucier

Ocean provided for me, I continued to think, read, gaze, wonder and try to place things into perspective. In my search, I read a quote from e. e. cummings that was of great comfort to me:

"For whatever we lose (like a you or a me).
It's always our self we find in the sea."

I watched the tides come and go, in and out, up and down. Every six hours the ocean would change its course. Perhaps it was time for me to do the same; suddenly, out of the blue, it hit me!

If it works for the sea, it will work for me!

Those words just couldn't have been more perfect.

I finally found me. I would never forget that Bob took from me the one true love of my life, nor did I feel I could ever forgive him. But, I found me. I would never forget that Matthew did not choose me, but I did understand that his love for me was not quite deep enough to make me the most important person in his life—that person remained Matthew. But, I found me.

It was at that moment that I decided to take my life back. I gathered up my books, realized that I had energy to spare and climbed the steep banking as opposed to taking the stairs up to the cottage. That was the turning point, the moment of my return to the days of fun, frills and friends. It was once again, time to play, to jet set and to enjoy the camaraderie of those whom I had turned into strangers. I began at the beginning, so, over the porch railing went the white towel.

The first to return to the fold was Lois. She had a dry sense of humor that was second to none with an imagination to match. She was the ideal person to be the first to get me back on the treadmill of our social life. Because she was intuitive and politically correct, I knew that she'd respect where I had been and that she wouldn't probe.

I rejoiced at the sound of Lois' motorboat making its way across the bay. I couldn't wait to see my old friend again. I had read her correctly. She didn't utter a word about her suspicions of what had happened between Matthew and me.

I was back and in style. Friends began coming around again. Although there was little time left before the start of the school year, we never missed a beat. The fall weekends were absolutely beautiful, and we took full advantage of them. The sailboat was out nearly every good weekend. Lois was aboard most of the time, while other passengers were mixed and matched.

The only tangible recreational piece of my past that I was willing to have as part of my renewed life was the sailboat. My powerboat never left the mooring for the remainder of the season except to be driven to the boatyard to be dry-docked for the winter. And I hired someone to do that. I just never could bring myself to board that boat again. The following spring I sold it. Life as it was on that boat would be frozen in time. I, personally, would never again sail that vessel.

With little effort, I managed to continue to keep my secret hidden—for now.

CHAPTER 17

This trip home from New York just never seemed to end, I thought as I drifted out of my daydreaming state for a reality check. Sadly enough, nothing much had changed. Matthew was still totally silent as he had been from the time we had left Queens. All indications were that he would maintain that state until we reached home. I looked down at my watch. Time was passing ever so slowly.

I was uncomfortable and feeling hungry—very, very hungry. I hadn't eaten anything since last night, nor had I had anything to drink with the exception of a sip of water that I gulped down before we left New York. I wasn't about to speak to Matthew—in fear that I would fall on deaf ears. I wasn't at all certain that I could handle any more rejection, whatever form, so I said nothing.

I usually carried a package of peanut butter snacking crackers in my purse. It was an old habit that I had developed because I spent so much time on the road. Fortunately, today was no different. Not only did I have one package, but there were two! Without saying a word, I placed one package on the seat between us and proceeded to open the other. Once I'd eaten, I felt so much better. Matthew didn't touch the package.

Although I so needed something wet to quench my thirst, I quickly resigned myself to the fact that there would be no beverage. I changed my position, closed my eyes and picked up where I had left off.

Summer had ended. The Brunswick house would come alive once again. Kay had returned from Islesboro, Sarah from Augusta and I had traveled the few miles from Blackstone. That first night home was like a homecoming celebration with never-ending tales of the happenings of the past summer. I said the least, and neither

J. C. Soucier

of my housemates asked questions. In another couple of days the school routine would shift into gear, back to the usual for everyone—except me.

Things would be very different now. My day would not include my usual detour to Jeanne's home. I hadn't spoken with her since the summer's episode with Bob. My day would not include the laughter and light-heartedness of Matthew's stories. My day would not include Matthew---nor would my evenings---nor would my weekends---nor would my life.

Day One of the school year was uneventful. Following a brief visit with my parents, I headed home to make dinner for my housemates, Kay and Sarah. When I arrived, I saw a huge bouquet of wild flowers sitting smack dab in the middle of the small side porch. I looked for a card, any indication of who this lovely surprise was for and from. There, beneath a green leaf was a card. On the envelope was written the name "Kate."

Taking a deep breath, I was unsure as to whether or not to open and read the message. I just knew it was from Matthew. Why would he do this? It was over. He had called it. We hadn't spoken in weeks, and I was beginning to do just fine, so why now? All of a sudden, for whatever reason, I unintentionally summoned the memories and the pain of that fateful day. I relived, in very few minutes, the heartbreaking experience that I somehow had survived not so long ago.

Sitting on the stoop, I leaned against the railing and looked up into the sky. The heavens were so beautiful. Those huge, puffy, pure white, cumulus clouds seemed strategically placed as they floated ever so slowly. I was drawing energy and inner peace from just taking this natural sedative. "Mother Nature seems to handle everything with such poise and elegance," I thought, "so shall I!"

In one swoop, I had risen, picked up the flowers and headed for the corner of the fence that surrounded the yard within which was a huge, four-sided cage. This was the cats' playground. That structure allowed the two cats (one mine and one Sarah's), to romp and play outdoors and at the same time kept them totally protected from the threat of other animals. Without a second thought, I nestled the stems of the flowers against the wood, wrapped the lovely purple ribbon around the wooden corner stake and tied a knot that was totally invisible to the naked eye. I stepped back to glance at my masterpiece and smiled.

"We'll make a good team no matter how far apart we are," I thought. "Thank you for the beautiful flowers, Matthew. I know that you mean well and that you're concerned. But, it's time to move on—so, I share your thoughtfulness with the world; however, your personal message will remain known only to you."

As I repeated those words I walked into the house. I turned to take one last look at the magnificent arrangement of flowers, unclenched my hand that held the card that was still in the envelope, tore it into pieces and dropped the tiny sections into the wastepaper basket.

CHAPTER 18

Feeling some back discomfort, I twisted and turned in my seat in an attempt to change my position and find something a little more comfortable. I leaned a little to the left and turned my shoulders slightly toward Matthew. He didn't flinch. He didn't look at me. His expression never changed. He didn't say a word. It was as though a robot was sitting behind that wheel, a true mechanical robot.

Somewhat accustomed to the chill in the air, I felt myself drifting back into the treasure box that held all those memories. Although some of the recollections were not totally happy experiences, they had all been part of building toward today—and on that note, I began revisiting.

For several weeks, Matthew used every method known to man to contact me. I avoided them all. Lovely flowers continued to be delivered. Totally ignored by me, the bouquets were too beautiful to throw away, so Sarah took them to school and placed them in the teachers' lounge. A card would arrive almost daily in the mail. When I returned from school, I'd pick it up from the sofa table, tear it and drop it into the trash. And of course, there was the telephone. I was always unavailable. Matthew kept trying and my housemates never gave in.

Suddenly, everything came to an abrupt stop. Flowers were no longer being delivered, the cards stopped coming and the telephone became silent. The last page had been written and the chapter had ended. But would that complete the book?

Christmas was just around the corner. Kay, Sarah and I were making our traditional holiday visits on Sunday, December 20, 1970. Every year, we would choose one Sunday when from morning 'til night, we would make our brief goodwill visit to friends' homes and deliver a little Christmas cheer. It was late afternoon, and we had two more stops to make. Kay was driving. Out of the clear blue sky and in a solemn whisper, I said:

"Kay, would you please drop me off at home?"

Uncertain of what she had heard, Kay responded, "Excuse me?"

"Would you please take me home—I don't know why, I just really need to go home."

Without any further discussion, Kay changed direction and headed back home. Because that was totally out of character for me, I'm certain that she felt the urgency in my request. Not a word was said about our change of plans, she simply drove directly home. As we walked into the house, the phone was ringing. Sarah answered, "Certainly, just a moment, please," she said. "It's for you—it's your cousin."

"My cousin?" I said with astonishment and disbelief. Something must be wrong.

"Kate, this is Jeanne. Come home right away. Your dad has fallen."

"Fallen? Is he okay?" I asked.

"Just come right home," Jeanne said. "Come right home."

"I'll be there as soon as I possibly can. Tell him, okay?" In a total daze, somehow I hung up the phone.

"It's my dad—he's fallen. I need to go home, now."

I ran up to my room and grabbed clothes at random.

"I'll never be back here to live, so I'll get everything out later, okay?"

"You'll be back, Kate. Your dad will be fine," said Kay.

"No, Kay, he won't be fine. My dad is dead. I just know it." Deep down in my heart I knew that my father had died. I would now move into my parent's home to care for my mother.

Kay and Sarah were not about to let me drive home alone. By the time I got out to my car, Kay was behind the wheel and Sarah was taking a second vehicle that would return them home. Within moments, we were en route.

As we headed out of Brunswick, a huge fire had broken out in a building just across the river on Route 217. Traffic was backed up for several miles, and we were caught in the middle of it. Feeling totally helpless and captive, I began to sob. I wanted so to be at my father's side. What if he hadn't passed away and he needed me? I just had to get home. Absolutely nothing was moving—cars were bumper to bumper, movement at a standstill.

"Please, please God, get me home. I must get to my dad, please!" I cried out. Suddenly, I heard a familiar voice,

"Hey!" I looked up and I saw my neighbor coming toward the car. He was a state trooper and had been called in to help control traffic. I opened the car door and ran to his side.

"Lou, Lou...please, my father...I need to get home..." I said sobbing. Kay had followed behind me and filled in the blanks, sharing the details with him.

"This is what we'll do," he said. "I'll take Kate home in the cruiser. When you guys get loose from this traffic jam, turn around as soon as you can and take the back road as an alternate route. I'll take care of Kate." Before I realized it, everything had been settled and we were heading home...fast.

Getting to Lewiston seemed to take forever. As we made the turn on the street where my parents were living, I saw a hearse coming toward us. My heart sank as my eyes swelled with tears. The conversation that I had with my dad the night before was to have been the last—ever, because I just knew that he was being carried in that hearse.

We'd spoken just last night, I thought. I love my Dad so. Now that I think about it, my father pretty much dominated that conversation. Usually the chat is an even exchange but last night, my dad's message was quite final. I didn't realize it at the time but now I'm wondering if he didn't have a significant purpose to his directives.

"Baby, you're going to make it in this world. You've got what it takes. I am so proud of you. Always remember how much I love you, and never forget that you were a chosen child. That makes you very special. Assure me that you will forever hear my voice whispering to you."

"I promise, Daddy, I promise."

"Good Kate, I'll take that vow to my grave so lock that away in your heart. Goodnight, Baby, sleep well."

I knew, deep down in my heart, that I would never hear my Dad's voice again. I also knew, deep down in my heart, that he was in that hearse that we had passed.

Bill Jones, the funeral director, was a good friend of my father's; he visited with him often. He drove two different vehicles; a Citron, which was his personal toy and what he drove socially, and a Cadillac, which he only took for business. The Cadillac was parked in front of the house when we arrived, a sight which I dreaded because it only confirmed that my father and my very best friend were gone forever.

Bill opened the door as I entered my parents' home. I collapsed into his arms. Once I had regained my composure I spotted my mother, sitting in her wheelchair at the far end of the table, sobbing. Her sister and niece were on either side of her, trying to console her. I went to her and held her in my arms. Tears were streaming down her cheeks

"Mother, I am so sorry, so sorry," I said. "We'll be okay, Dad promised," and I cried, and cried and cried.

My mother was upset not only over having lost her life long partner but because she felt that somehow, she should have been able to save him when he fell to the floor, directly in front of her wheelchair.

"He fell right here at my feet Kate; I was trapped in the corner of this kitchen and couldn't get help for him. By the time I moved him and got to the phone, he had died. I tried, I tried to help him." My parents had been entertaining that afternoon. Within minutes after their guests had left, my dad fell diagonally across the kitchen floor trapping my mother's wheelchair in the corner. She actually moved his body over enough to make it past him and get to the telephone. She called my cousin, Jeanne, who was a registered nurse. Jeanne immediately called the ambulance and then rushed to the house.

"He died of a massive coronary, and it was instant; no one could have revived him, he was gone before he fell to the floor." the doctor told my mother. Those words were consoling to me. At least he hadn't suffered. It sounded like he never knew – but then, from his conversation with me last night, he knew.

Crazy things happen when this kind of tragedy strikes a family. For example, thoughts crossed my mind that my dad had orchestrated the timing of his death. He knew that I would have fallen apart if I would have walked in to see him lying lifeless on the floor. He had been removed only minutes before I arrived. Being the good natured, bargainer that he was, I can imagine him negotiating with God---probably saying something like:

"I'll go peacefully if you'll promise to get me out of Dodge before my daughter walks through the door." I smiled. Even at a time like this, my Dad dominated the situation and through it all, he managed to send me a message that I interpreted as being, "Don't be sad, Baby, we've had a great life and created wonderful memories---carry on and make me proud." That was his style...his way...his gentle way.

People traffic, people traffic, people traffic—well meaning people were in and out of the house much of the night, offering to help, extending their sorrow. I wandered around in a bit of a haze. I spoke with folks, and it seemed like every time someone new would arrive, the crying would start all over again. Just as I thought I had things in check, the door would open and the gates of hell would release. Although exhausted, I had no choice; I needed to continue meeting and greeting guests. My dad would expect that of me, he'd already made it clear; he had always been a gracious host, welcoming each individual in a personal, unique way. Now it was my turn.

At one point, the door swung open, luggage entered first and my Aunt Louise, my dad's sister-in-law, followed. Recently widowed in June, she was still very close to the pain of losing a precious person. She now wanted to give back some of that comfort that my father had given her. A Lucille Ball sort of character by nature, her wit would certainly help lighten the burden. Her timing was perfect. She was the ideal remedy for this prelude into mourning the death of my dad whom I adored.

Being an only child with a mother who was afflicted with MS and thereby restricted and totally dependent, I retired that night knowing that I would awake to having to deal with the reality of my father's eternal departure. I just couldn't imagine a day without him. I lay in bed and fought ever so hard to stay awake—I didn't want to fall asleep and awake to the reality that awaited me. In spite of my efforts, I could feel the heaviness of my eyes making them close as tears continued falling on my pillow. With my final conscious breath I called out, "Daddy—Daddy?"

He didn't answer.

CHAPTER 19

The following morning I saw the sunrise. I wished so hard to have that moment frozen in time and never to have to move forward.

Please don't let another minute go by, I whispered to myself, I just can't make arrangements to bury my dad. Although a family friend owned the funeral parlor, it didn't make having to work out those details any easier. The casket—how could I ever pick out a casket? How could I choose a container that would eternally hold my father? It was so final. I just couldn't bring myself to think about it, let alone envision doing it! Where would I get the strength to carry on? What were my options?

I moved to the chair by a window that overlooked a small backyard that was being covered with a blanket of pure white falling snow. I knew that I would have to do it all. For survival purposes and because my heart and mind were so overloaded, I had to disengage one of them and I chose my heart. It was the only way that I could preserve myself and gather strength.

Wouldn't you know we were having a snowstorm? My dad loved that kind of weather. When I was a little girl, he and I would sit together and watch storms. He'd even wake me in the middle of the night, make hot chocolate and we'd spend hours watching snowflakes float gently to the ground or be driven fiercely by the force of nature. My dad would say, "Nature is Mother Earth, governess of the world. Respecting her precious gifts is very, very important, Baby. So together we'll do it!" And we'd sip our hot chocolate in her honor.

Leaving it all behind, the matter at hand was that I had to prepare to make funeral arrangements. I must get his favorite suit, tie, socks and shoes. I knew the outfit that he had planned to wear on

J. C. Soucier

Christmas. I'll get that together. And his watch—yes, his watch...

For his last birthday, I had given my father a gold pocket watch engraved with the words:

> Daddy
> I Love You
> Kate

He had kept it in its original box for fear of losing it before he received the gold chain that he knew I was giving him this Christmas. Sadly, I never got the chance to give him the second part of his gift, and so, to my knowledge, he'd never worn the watch. But he would. I had the chain and he would wear his watch piece in his casket.

Once my mother was up and about, I went into her bedroom and to the dresser where my dad kept his jewelry. I opened the drawer, took the velvet box and opened it. No watch. He must have put it elsewhere and I was certain that my mother would know where. I went into the kitchen and asked her.

"Why he never took it out of the velvet box, Kate. It should be in the top drawer of his dresser. Now that I think about it, he just mentioned the other day that he couldn't wait to wear it at Christmas. He was so proud of that watch that you gave him."

Well, it wasn't in the box in the drawer and neither was the velvet pouch. I didn't want to upset my mother by telling her that I had already checked and didn't find it there. For now, I let it go.

I took a quick shower hoping that it would energize me to meet the challenges of the day. It wasn't quite 7 a.m. While the coffee was perking, I decided I would go out and pick up doughnuts and coffee cakes since I expected that people were going to begin dropping by early.

Out and back in a jiffy, I returned shortly before our first visitor. As my mother, aunt and I were sitting around the breakfast table, we heard stomping footsteps followed by rather rambunctious knocks at the door. As I turned to welcome our guest, the door flew open and Matthew entered. He took me into his arms saying:

"Kate, my darling Kate," he whispered softly, "I am so, so

sorry." He held me tight. His embrace was so comforting to me; I broke down and began crying uncontrollably.

"I will take care of all the formal arrangements for you, Kate. No need to worry."

I continued to cry. I needed Matthew so much that very moment and he was there. He knew how much my Dad meant to me and although he wasn't able to comfort me openly as Matthew, he smoothly transitioned into his role as Father Matt and provided me with exactly what I needed at that time.

Time elapsed and the emotions began to lighten up. All four of us were now at the table having coffee and breakfast. My aunt, though not intentionally, was being humorous, and that helped make the beginning of the first day without my father at least a little tolerable.

It wasn't very long before my mother's brother, Charles, arrived. He was another blessing. He offered to accompany me to the funeral parlor. So, there it was: Matthew was going to handle the formalities of the service and Uncle Charles would be there to help me with the details of the preparations for my dad's final sendoff. My father had never left me in a lurch before and he wasn't going to start now. That was the first time since he died that I felt some sort of comfort and security. I raised my eyes to the heavens and said so only my father could hear… Thank you, Daddy.

Although the snow was falling steadily, by 8:30 that morning the house had filled with additional relatives, friends and neighbors. My aunt was there to handle things; Kay and Sarah had come back to help as well. The time had come to do the inevitable, to go to the funeral parlor to meet with Bill and finalize arrangements. Bill had spoken to me the night before and said that he would await my arrival and that time wasn't a factor. I wish I could have waited forever, but I knew only too well that the longer I delayed, the more difficult it would be. If I needed to walk through hell, I decided to speed up the pace. I caught my Uncle Charles' attention and nodded to leave. Within moments, we put on our jackets, wrapped scarves around our necks and trudged through the snow to his car.

J. C. Soucier

Uncle Charles drove his Buick to the back door entrance. Bill was waiting for us. As I entered, he hugged me.

"I am so sorry for your loss, Kate. Your father was a wonderful father to you and a best friend to me. I'll try to make this as easy for you as possible, dear. Your dad already did most of the work to spare you at this difficult time."

We walked directly into his office and Bill led me to a very beautiful, oriental chair that faced his hand-carved teakwood desk. My uncle sat next to me.

The process needed to begin. Questions needed to be answered. More questions needing more answers. When would you like visiting hours? Which day will you want the burial? What time do you want mass? Which Church? Who will celebrate mass? Do you have pall bearers? Did you bring his clothes?

"According to your dad, Kate, these were his wishes: Day One would be for immediate family only. Day Two would be visiting hours for friends and family. Day Three would be burial day. He gave me a list of who he would like to have asked to be pall bearers and that you would decide who the priest would be for it all. You just need to agree to fulfill his wishes."

"Okay, absolutely, I want his final wishes to be followed to the letter. He planned it all. As for the priest, Father Matthew will be in touch with you." My dad knew all along about Matthew and me, this was his way of telling me that. He just knew.

Before leaving I suddenly realized that I had left my dad's clothes behind.

"I forgot his clothes. I'm so sorry, Bill, I'll bring those to you later this morning."

"I'll bring them back, Bill," said Uncle Charles. "When I take you home, Kate, if you'll give them to me, I'll bring them right back."

"Thank you, Uncle Charles, will that be alright, Bill?"

"Fine," he answered.

Now we had to deal with choosing a casket, the moment that I dreaded the very most.

"What about the casket, Bill?"

"Your father has chosen his casket, Kate. Shortly after his first heart attack he gave me all the details that I just shared with you and he came here on what he called his last shopping spree. That's all set and you don't have to deal with that at all." My dad knew how to do things and how to continue to protect me, even after he was gone. Again, thank you, Daddy!

It was over. All the funeral arrangements to lay my father to eternal sleep had been discussed and finalized. All that was left to do was to choose flower arrangements from my mother and from me. A single red rose that would be placed beside his head in his casket was going to be my choice. That would make him happy---a single red rose that would be with him forever.

I stood up to leave and Bill handed me a large plastic bag that had the clothes that my dad was wearing when he died and a smaller plastic bag that carried articles from his pockets. Immediately I spotted the velvet pouch that was bulging with what I knew was my father's gold pocket watch. Very surprised I asked, "Where did this gold watch come from, Bill?

"It was in your father's back pocket."

Puzzled, I thought of what my father had told me repeatedly, that his watch was not going to leave the safety of its box until he received his gold chain. Is it possible that he had a premonition of his death and wanted to wear his treasured piece just once?

You know, it always seemed to me that he had an uncanny, sort of mysterious ability to just know things. He never predicted the existence or happening of an experience, but would often say or do things that when looking back, would have a direct connection. Whether he had psychic ability, was a little avant-garde or it was all just coincidental, no one will ever know.

CHAPTER 20

On December 23, 1970, we buried my dad. Maine had been hit by a huge snowstorm. It had been snowing for three days. Although this storm was gentle and very beautiful, that white stuff was persistent and relentless about piling up. On Wednesday morning, the setting for my father's final journey home could not have been more perfect.

I could just hear him saying, "Take a good look, Baby, this is what heaven looks like."

In spite of the storm, the Cathedral was filled with a multitude of people who had come to bid their last farewell to a gentle, generous man whose occasional roar of a lion was part of his antics. Among those in attendance was a group of staff and children from the local orphanage. They had braved the storm to represent the home where my dad delivered gifts for the children every Christmas Eve. He had wanted to remain anonymous and did, until my Uncle Charles made the discovery. He found bags of gifts filled with toys stored at the drycleaners. Attached to one of the bags was a tag that had the number of boys, number of girls and name and address of the home. Upon contacting the director of the home, the story unfolded. The very first time my mother and I had heard of this was during my uncle's eulogy when he shared this legend.

Due to the severity of the storm, I asked Matthew to make arrangements for a brief gathering in the entrance of the Church in lieu of people driving to the cemetery. Only the immediate family in chauffeured limousines would travel the distance. At the end of the mass, Matthew invited everyone to join him in the foyer of the church for this impromptu gathering as he made reference to how this spontaneous change reflected my father's impish character.

I had chosen the Ode of Joy as the recessional song because it really reflected my father. The aisle of the cathedral seemed endless as I walked directly behind my dad's casket making our way to the entrance. Friends and family assembled to say their last goodbye; a comforting exercise for me to bear witness to the wonderful tribute being given to my hero, my dad.

Following the brief committal ceremony at the cemetery, I returned home to a houseful of guests waiting to join in the celebration of a man who absolutely cherished life and so loved Christmas. We would decorate from top to bottom every year, except this year, we ran out of time. After his heart attack, he had been very restricted in what he could do for activities; therefore, we had agreed that under his supervision, I would put up the tree and all other decorations when I came home for the holidays on December 21. He didn't quite make it. He died on December 20.

In spite of the intensity of the storm, the house was overflowing with guests. Another crazy, rather wild idea crossed my mind. "Let's decorate," I thought, "wouldn't my dad just beam at this off the wall idea!" And so, I invited everyone to join me in that activity. My mother was appalled at my action. That, however, didn't stop me from pursuing what I truly believed would put a smile on my father's face that would beam from ear to ear! My Aunt Louise fell right into cadence and was my mother's restitution to help her maintain her sanity in all of this. Meanwhile, I recruited Kay, Sarah and Jeanne to help me implement this insane plan. Within minutes, word had circulated and I began delegating jobs. A few of the men went to the attic to dig out the decorations, someone else went to the garage to bring in the live tree that my father had purchased and stored and others were beginning to rearrange the living room, preparing it to become the center of the celebration. A few new items had been purchased with which to decorate and people were busy opening those packages. The record player was playing Christmas music, and together we celebrated the life of a man whose spirit would never die.

By nightfall, the house was decorated as it had never been before. A Christmas tree whose bright shining star touched the ceiling was dressed with hundreds of lights and brilliant decorations that my dad loved so much. I had mounted and framed his obituary and it hung gracefully from the base of the star on the tree. Fresh holly garland swags were swirled throughout the house. Triads of electric candles were placed on all the windowsills. Vibrant poinsettia wreaths adorned both doors. Fresh flower arrangements, plants and centerpieces brought such life to the house. My dad would have loved it! I could just hear him saying,

"Great party, Baby, you're a chip off the old block!"

About 10 p.m., guests began to leave. We had certainly given my dad the sendoff that he so deserved. He loved a party. We found great comfort from our family and friends, even my mother conceded that her spirits had been lifted.

By Christmas Eve the weather had not improved. Roads were impassable to the point where hospitals were asking for anyone who had snow sleds to help transport doctors, nurses and other hospital personnel to and from the facility. For many years, our family gathered at Bob and Jeanne's on Christmas Eve. The plan remained unchanged. Although my mother had no intention of leaving the house and celebrating. She preferred to stay home and mourn my dad. Although she never said a word, I think that she had not completely forgiven me and was still trying to digest the Christmas decorations that filled our home with spirit. Taking charge, I refused to have us spend Christmas at home, alone. In spite of the hurt that I suffered as a result of Bob's indiscretion and bizarre behavior, I had chosen to bury that history with my dad and had made arrangements with Jeanne to have the men hook up a sled behind one of the snowmobiles and come for us. We were about one quarter of a mile from one another.

About four o'clock on Christmas Eve a racket was heard coming from the ramped porch on the side of the house. Moments later, in came Bob and Pete, ready to transport my mother and me on the sled. With little resistance, my mother agreed to take an adventure ride. Wrapped in a fur coat, hat and mittens that my dad had bought her for Christmas, Bob and Arnie picked her up and sat her in the sled. With a heavy blanket, I tightly bundled her up like a mummy, wrapping her scarf loosely over her mouth and around her face. She wore glasses to protect her eyes from the blowing snow. Collapsing her wheelchair, I placed it between myself and

J. C. Soucier

the sled as I stood on the back runners, hanging on for dear life. We were ready to go!

Bob carefully made his way down the ramp and into the driveway. Nothing was moving. There wasn't evidence or tracks of anything having passed. Even city snowplows hadn't been through. Snowdrifts were piled high as we slowly made our way, down and around the challenging sculptured roads and mounds of snow.

Although it took nearly a half hour, we finally made it. My mother was so excited about the adventure ride she had just experienced that she was smiling from ear-to-ear and her bright red cheeks and green eyes had life in them again. The challenging weather that my dad loved brought a few moments of comfort to my mother. He left in style. Thanks, Daddy.

Christmas 1970 came and went. I missed my father terribly— but his strength gave us the spirit that dominated the holidays as we celebrated in his memory.

CHAPTER 21

I relocated to my mother's home, lock, stock and barrel. Matthew re-entered my life. Every evening, my mother would settle into bed about nine o'clock. Shortly thereafter, Matthew would come to visit. Our relationship picked up as though nothing had ever happened. The love that had been inhumanly ripped away from us some four and half months before had found its way back.

Winter was in full bloom and it was a record year for snow. The ski resorts were prospering as skiers headed there in multitudes. Matthew and I were among the enthusiasts. Gretchen, the housekeeper-companion to my mother, was a wonderful German lady who very willingly would spend nights at our home whenever I wanted a break.

Matthew took time during February school break and rented an A-frame at Sugarloaf for a week. Both of us were avid skiers and wasted no time hitting the slopes when the lifts began running every morning. We'd ski until four o'clock when the mountain closed. After taking a quick shower, Matthew and I would settle in for a nice dinner and dreamy evening in our cozy rented abode with an open loft over half of the building; the remainder was wide open from floor to the very tip of the vaulted ceiling. Finished in shiny, knotty pine with wooden pegs, the inside lent itself to nurturing a relationship that, although unspoken, was recovering from a terrible injury. The warm glow of the flickering flames in the fireplace engulfed and enhanced an already existing romantic ambience.

We would occasionally make reference to our time apart, but these occasions were few and far between. The concern that I constantly harbored was that of history repeating itself.

J. C. Soucier

"How long this time before once again we are torn apart?" I would ask. It felt so perfect, why was I so scared?

And to that Matthew would say, "It will never happen again, Kate. Our love is far too beautiful and far too deep to succumb to any pressure. Our love will survive any destructive efforts by the most powerful of humans."

He was convincing, and I so wanted to believe him. But why then couldn't I shake the feeling that something somewhere was lurking in the shadows of our relationship?

Matthew would periodically suggest that I was becoming paranoid and needed to put my energies into trusting him – and so, I bowed to the power and let go.

CHAPTER 22

Time for another reality check, and we were not yet home. 3 p.m. was what my watch said. We still had many miles to go. Memories that were coming back to me were bittersweet. There had been the good times and the not so good times, but none compared to the experience that I'd had earlier this morning.

I needed to get back to my safety zone. It was keeping me somewhat comfortable and able to make this horrendous trip back without breaking down. Nothing in the immediate, real picture had changed. Matthew still had not broken his silence. So I drifted back to 1971, because '71 had been a very good year.

The winter of 1970 had come and gone. After losing my dad, regaining Matthew turned the next months into a magical time. I had become the proud owner of a beautiful Siberian husky female puppy that I loved so much. Sabrina was her name. She protected me, she comforted me, and she was my special buddy. It took a little while for Sabrina and Matthew to hit it off. She needed to be constantly at my side and Matthew had to share his space. In spite of this challenge, Matthew and my relationship seemed greater than ever. Unlike other couples in love, we had to celebrate privately because the secret that we shared needed to be protected. Today, I wonder exactly how much the secretiveness and forbidden status of the relationship were the driving forces that kept the two of us together.

Spring had sprung. Gretchen had agreed to move in with my mother for the summer, making it possible for me to live at the cottage. School ended, and the transition from home to Blackstone was quickly made. This time, plans were that the summer home would accommodate two and my dog.

J. C. Soucier

Matthew, still circulating within the original group of friends that included Bob, maintained his routine of periodic visits. His focus however, had become me and keeping the second very secret life, intact.

In preparation for summer, the cottage had to be opened, water hooked up and a thorough cleaning had to be done. A quick call to the marina scheduling a date for the boat to be launched would take care of the sailboat. That process included washing it down, filling the water tank and making it shine like the diamond of the sea that it would be. The sails had been washed and thoroughly dried before being stored, so they were ready. Soon we'd be set to sail all over again.

It was a bit ironic that last summer our love aboard a power boat reflected that loud, explosive drama that we experienced; this summer, our relationship would take on a more silent, demure stature, somewhat like the sailboat that we would enjoy.

The move to the cottage was made. Matthew commuted daily, seeming to have no accountability to his priestly duties except saying mass and hearing confession. He occasionally had an appointment or two with parishioners who needed his guidance, but he referred most of these people to other priests. He also managed to take several days off in succession every week; we took advantage of those combinations and sailed off into the horizon for overnights.

The three of us (Sabrina was included) spent hours of darkness anchored in various coves surrounded by the mystery of these enchanted islands. Night after night we would swim in the moonlight, hearing only the sound of water splashing against our bodies. We slept to the rhythm of the waves rocking the boat and awoke to the sound of birds singing and porpoises splashing. Even on drizzly nights, the sound of lightly falling rain was soothing. When the fog rolled in and held us captive, the eeriness and mystery of the unknown was enchanting. There was such elusiveness about the ocean; it was ambiguous, indistinct and ever so vague. To disrespect the sea was to ignore its power to dominate, control and govern. The ocean, so vast and blue, was a sanctuary for those of us who loved her.

Perfect

Although I was happy, I couldn't help being tormented periodically by the threat that someday, this would all come to an end. I hadn't let go altogether, but I was constantly working toward the day when I no longer would give losing Matthew a thought. Finally, the day arrived! I decided to live in the moment and life took on a whole different perspective.

How delightful were our experiences together. We had breakfast onboard under the warm summer sun, took a morning swim into shore to explore the beach, climbed along the rocky coast of Maine and dug our feet into the few sandy sections of the coves. We picked up little treasures perhaps with the intention that they would forever be remembrances of these times together.

Perhaps because every day was so precious, the summer seemed to pass ever so quickly. Suddenly we awoke one day and it was time to move back to the city. Having to leave the cottage this particular fall was very difficult because it meant more than just physically relocating. It meant giving up an absolutely love-filled lifestyle at Blackstone that had been tailored for Matthew, Sabrina and me. It meant leaving behind all the enhancements that had made our love so very magical. We would have to return to protecting the secrecy of our partnership, calculating our every move, constantly being on the lookout for any sign of someone lurking in the shadows, controlling our emotions and reactions toward one another when in public together and giving up the wonderful freedom that we had so appreciated because our time together would be isolated, at least for now.

To make all of this even more challenging, the geographical distance between the rectory and where I was living was less than a mile; Bob and Jeanne were two streets away, and my Aunt Julia was my neighbor. The Garden of Eden was in everyone's backyard.

Although our lifestyle changed drastically, Matthew and I both adapted very quickly to the way things had to be. Matthew would visit every night after his parish duties had been completed. Still, my mother's bedtime preceded his arrival by nearly one hour. Although never physically seeing Matthew in the house all of those evenings, her discreetness about his presence remained her private information that she took to her grave.

Sabrina's behavior was perfect as she didn't make a sound to announce his arrival. It was almost as though she knew that the secret of our relationship was private and had to be protected. So the sound of Matthew's car turning into the driveway was not an alarm to her and it was music to my ears. Every evening I longed to hear the hum of that engine. He was a food lover and I very much enjoyed surprising him with a different combination of snacks and hors d'oeuvres. He never knew from one night to another what would be served, and that was pretty adventurous for us both. As I look back on all of this, I wonder now how many neighbors were really fooled by this same vehicle parking close to the house every night in an attempt to conceal its presence. I'm thinking that we were the only ones who were fooled in thinking that our secret was a secret. But it worked for us at the time.

Each evening, Matthew's arrival was a production because he was so dramatic. He'd enter the house with flair; his hand would pull the white plastic collar out of the slits in his shirt and he would automatically tuck it into his left breast pocket. His arms would then reach out to embrace the woman he loved as he tenderly and passionately kissed me hello.

That led to snacking, usually in the family room where a small table was set up. Music and soft lights gave the room a golden glow. A dance or two before eating would often take precedence. The time would come to introduce Matthew to the recipe of the night, and that was always fun. Many of these culinary experiences were unforgettable for him. For instance, the evening that I served Matthew escargots dipped in garlic sauce was a trip that he took by himself. I had a sandwich that night—I remember it well. In spite of it all, no matter what was on the serving platter, the presentation was unique and colorful. The one ingredient that was common in every one of these dishes was love, and that was very obvious.

Just to add a little humor to the mix, Matthew was almost as huge a hot chocolate fan as I was. To stir things up a little, and not to leave simple hot chocolate unadulterated, I sweetened the pot by stirring the hot chocolate with a peppermint candy cane. Instant addiction for us both! From that point on, hot chocolate with a candy cane stirrer was a must as Matthew, Sabrina and I became addicted to the *Tonight Show* with Johnny Carson.

We ate, we talked, we danced, we loved, we laughed, we played board games, we sipped on hot chocolate with melted peppermint candy canes, we watched the *Tonight Show*... Our nightly rendezvous were never, ever boring!

At 1 a.m., when Johnny Carson signed off, Matthew would leave and return to the rectory. Minutes after his arrival, my phone would ring. Although we had just left one another, we always seemed to have more to say that would take up another half to full hour of conversation. After hanging up, I would lay there with my eyes wide open, Sabrina by my side, afraid that any minute I would awake and discover that this was a myth, a fabrication of my imagination, a dream that would vanish.

I often carried being mesmerized by this man into the next day. In spite of the few hours of sleep, I would be up bright and early ready to handle whatever the day had to offer. It was as though I was bouncing from one huge puffy cloud to another surrounded by bright sunshine and lots of fresh air. My mind would often wander to the night before and I'm certain that the smile of pure contentment on my face had to make people wonder what I was up to. No one ever asked and I certainly didn't offer any explanation.

CHAPTER 23

It was early in December of 1971. Matthew was preparing to leave for Italy. He and priest friends were traveling before the intensity of the Christmas holiday enveloped them.

Sabrina and I drove Matthew to the airport as we serenaded each other with "Arrivederci Roma." The fact that neither of us could carry a tune made the forty-mile trek quite humorous. I laughed and laughed until tears filled my eyes and Matthew roared a real old-fashioned belly laugh. What a wonderful way to leap into this much-dreaded two week separation period.

We arrived at the airport with plenty of time to spare. I pulled over into a widened area along the fence that separated the runway from the road. It was a beautiful night, the crescent moon was like a big smile in the sky and the runways were all lit up like Christmas trees.

"I'm going to miss you so, Kate—how wonderful it would be if we could take this trip together." Would we ever, I thought? Would we ever board a plane and head to Europe together?

"You'll have a grand time, Matthew; and between it all, I do hope that you miss me every single day. I'll be here waiting when you return."

We embraced. The windows got steamy. The noise of a landing plane jolted us into reality. After a quick glance down at his watch, Matthew took my face into his hands as he said, "It's time to go, Kate. As much as I hate to leave you, we must go."

The extra minutes had flown by, and check-in time for an international flight was two hours prior to boarding time. It was time to go. I drove to the proper entrance, Matthew got out, took his luggage and, because there was a chance of being within the scope of someone's watchful eye, he simply winked and softly whispered,

J. C. Soucier

"I love you very, very much, Kate. Love me." He smiled, turned and walked away.

As I drove away my eyes filled with tears. I was proud of myself because I had done so very well. I hadn't shed a tear. I wanted Matthew to leave excited about his trip as opposed to having sad thoughts of leaving me behind. This enabled me to give the man of my life a magnificent sendoff—and I did; it was an Oscar- winning performance.

I usually enjoyed the days' end when the sun would set and night would fall. Not seeing Matthew in the evening changed all of that. It was 9:30, just about the time that Matthew would usually arrive. I found myself having absolutely nothing to look forward to— no trial run of some new recipe, no anticipation of hearing that melodic sound of Matthew driving into the driveway, no sweet embrace as he would flamboyantly make his grand entrance, no romantic midnight snack, no laughter, no games. Even Johnny Carson wasn't inviting to watch that first night alone, or second, or third…

I was curled up on the divan, drinking a hot chocolate; that sensuous flavor and aroma of peppermint seemed to have a soothing, consoling effect on me. I could almost sense the touch of Matthew's arms around me and feel the warmth of his neck as I could just see myself cuddled up to him.

Sabrina was snuggled up to me as though she knew that I was feeling melancholy and all she wanted to do was comfort me. Unconditional love, I thought, the intimacy of a dog is based on unrestricted, never-ending love. Can a love between a man and a woman be that complete and eternal? Life without Matthew would be unbearable. It had happened once before, and inasmuch as he promised that we would never again be separated, what really was there to prevent similar steps from being taken again? Matthew talked so often of the power of love—we had reached a plateau in our relationship that was beyond destruction—how realistic was that, really? I had to believe him; that was my survival tool—complete, unwavering, solid trust in the man I so loved.

My trance was suddenly interrupted by the ringing of the telephone.

"I just wanted to say good morning to you, Kate, and that I miss you. Bet you've been watching Johnny Carson and he just bid you goodnight, right? Miss me?" Calling from across the sea, it was so good to hear Matthew's voice. It was 6 a.m. in Italy.

"I'll be home soon, and it will be as though we've never been apart. I think of you constantly, Kate. I love........." and the line went dead.

My heart was pounding so hard that I thought it was going to bounce right out of my chest. I didn't want to let go of the phone, so I held it tightly and fell asleep with it. I awoke hours later with it still clutched in my hand.

CHAPTER 24

and a Merry Christmas to all! It was the season!

Matthew had returned safely from his trip. The stories that he brought back were entertaining and never ending. His ability to embellish a tale made them even that much more delightful. Although the busyness and commitments of the Christmas holidays took up much of his time, in spite of it all, he managed to squeeze in a few late night visits. New Year's Eve was going to be the big night---our night. Although Matthew had to make a few goodwill visits early in the evening, he had promised to be with me when the clock struck midnight. He stayed true to his word.

By the same token, I planned to make the evening very special. I found recipes that undoubtedly would make food gurus water at the mouth and rush to add them to their selective menu of favorites. My only words of advice to Matthew were, "Please, eat only to be sociable because you need to arrive here with an empty belly."

"I should be with you about 9:30," Matthew said. "I must make three stops before wrapping it up, and I'll begin my visits as early as possible. So, let's plan our activities to begin about 9:45. I'll be on time, promise!"

He never was on time. It just wasn't part of Matthew's nature to be time sensitive. Add twenty minutes to whatever hour he gives as his estimated time of arrival was my rule of thumb, and I was pretty much on the mark most instances.

New Year's Eve, however, was different. Everything was ready. The table in the family room where we spent all of our time had been set to reflect the holiday. One would have never guessed that the gracefully draped red tablecloth was concealing a shaky card table. A textured green runner clearly defined the center point from which the pewter candelabra provided a soft glow, enhancing the romantic aura that enveloped the room.

TV trays were also cleverly decorated and their identity was hidden. They made terrific holding stations for additional dishes and covered plated courses. Everything was ready—and so was I!

I sat in the Boston rocker that was positioned in one corner of the room, just waiting to hear Matthew's car. It was nine o'clock, still a little early. Within moments, and very much to my surprise, I heard the melodic hum of his engine. I couldn't believe that Matthew was early! I jumped to my feet, barely able to contain my anxieties. Tonight was going to be our night. Together, we would bid farewell to 1971 and launch our dreams into 1972.

As Matthew walked through the door, the collar never made it to his pocket this time. Neither one of us had the patience to wait that extra moment for that process to occur. We passionately melted into one another's arms.

Dinner was delicious. Matthew told stories, we reminisced, we laughed and we danced. It was 11:30 before we finished our meal and antics. I had anticipated that we both would be full – absolutely full to overflowing therefore, I had not prepared any sweet dessert except of course, our traditional cup of hot chocolate enhanced by the flavor of a peppermint stick.

The time had come for most of the world to celebrate in unison, the retirement of one year and birth of another. The clock struck that magical hour of midnight as we passionately professed our love to one another. On New Year's Eve, so very much in love, we created what would later become this perfect combination's... perfect combination.

CHAPTER 25

It was a cold, late-February afternoon. School had been given an early release because of an unexpected snowstorm that had blanketed the city. Mom and I had been chatting and looking out the window, admiring the beautiful snowfall. The phone rang. I suspected that I knew the identity of the person on the other end of the phone and the purpose for the call; if that was the case, I needed to control how I responded to the anticipated news since my mother was but a few feet away. Without wanting to appear overly anxious, I slowly sauntered over to the table and answered the telephone.

"Hello," I said in a melodious, rich, alto voice. I was right.

"Congratulations, Kate, results of your pregnancy test are back and you are pregnant!" It was my doctor's nurse. Since I was standing but a few feet away from my mother, I ever so quietly expressed my appreciation for the call and made reference that I would call them back for an appointment. I wanted so very much to explode with excitement, but I really couldn't do that. I had to pretend that the caller was anyone but the nurse from the obstetrician's office. My mind governed my actions by forcefully dictating control. Fortunately, my mother was not inquisitive and didn't have a need to know every little thing. There was no further discussion about the call.

Inside though, inside—I was jumping with joy! Pregnant! I am pregnant! I am so pregnant! Yikes! I am so very, very happy! I kept repeating and repeating those words to myself in silence. It's a wonder that the smirk on my face didn't give me away. I couldn't tell my mother. Actually, I couldn't tell anyone. Not now anyway. How unfair was that? I wanted to climb the highest mountain and shout it to the world. But for now, I was the world. No one else could know except Matthew. I needed to tell him as soon as possible. That would happen tonight.

Well, tonight came. Although it was pretty much his regular time, it seemed like forever before Matthew arrived. I was bursting at the seams from having such difficulty restraining myself from announcing the news at the top of my voice! I just couldn't wait another moment to tell him. Finally, the door opened and in he came. The expression on my face along with my giddiness tipped him off that something was a little bit out of the ordinary. He went through his regular collar to the pocket routine and, never missing a beat, he scooped me up into his arms, a position that I had longed for all day. As he embraced me, I'm sure that he could feel my heart beating as though it was going to leap right out of my chest. That was it. I just couldn't hold this secret for one more second.

"Come, quickly. You need to sit down," I said taking his hand and leading the way into the family room.

"What's going on Kate? Your eyes are sparkling, your face is lit up like a neon sign, you're grinning from ear to ear and you're flitting around like a butterfly freshly out of her cocoon—what's happening?"

"Matthew, I am so happy, and so in love with you. I want...I hope...oh...I'm pregnant!"

"Pregnant?" Matthew repeated. "Are you sure?"

"Of course I'm sure. I had my pregnancy test in Dr. Martin's office and his nurse called this afternoon to tell me that the test came back positive. I can't wait to see the doctor himself. I'll call from school tomorrow to make my first appointment."

"Wait...wait, I...." said Matthew. "Don't rush into this now. No need to call the doctor's office as soon as tomorrow. Just wait..."

"Wait? Why wait? Aren't you excited about this baby, Matthew? You don't seem happy. I know that it's a bit of a shock, but is it a happy shock?" Matthew just sat there and didn't respond.

"I'm going to have our baby Matthew, isn't that the most wonderful news you could ever want to hear? Or...is it?"

"Great news Kate—great news. But we need to think about

this. We need to think about you, me, us, the baby. We need to think about what this will all mean," Matthew uttered in a very low, calm voice.

"What do you mean, Matthew? What do you mean by saying that we need to think about this? What exactly is there to think about except that I am pregnant and we begin there?"

"You need to think about us, me, Kate. I do love you, I love you with all my heart, but I am a priest."

"Newly ordained are you? Were you not a priest yesterday, the day before, all last summer and the summer before that? Suddenly the fact that you are a priest surfaces when all the time we talked about our relationship and your vocation, it was your justification that you were first born a man. Now it's opening night, Matthew— curtain is rising and you're center stage. What now?"

"I don't know…I'm…I just don't know."

"Look, that's perfectly fine, Matthew. Long ago I accepted this triangle, and I'm not competing. So please, don't put me in that position. From the beginning we both have known that we've been on a collision course; and we have navigated through the waters in spite of it all. It was a choice, a conscious choice. Now we face the music. And it's okay. It's really okay, Matthew because I truly believe that once a priest always a priest. I'll bow to the power. You remain a priest and I'll be a mother."

"Is it really that simple, Kate?" questioned Matthew.

"Yes, it can be. It can be that simple. Just don't complicate things. Let it be that simple."

"But you don't understand," said Matthew, "I will have to explain this to several people. What will I tell them?"

"I, too, may have some explaining to do; but only if I choose. Either way, we can keep it simple. Our relationship is very sacred to me, Matthew, and that will never change. You know, I've always felt that some day something would force us to go our separate ways in the physical sense of our life together. Maybe this will be the fork in the road. Although you will always be my only one true love, Matthew, perhaps our love is greater than what a mortal partnership has to offer. Maybe the depth of our devotion is meant to be shared just between the three of us---mother, father and child.

Whatever be the reason, whatever the ultimate result, things will be okay. We have shared far too much of our inner self with one another for this to become unbeautiful."

I so hoped that I could pull this off for both of us; I didn't want to lose Matthew, but, he couldn't know how devastated I would be should he chose the church to be his life-long partner. It was only fair because after all, his initial choice had been the church--- perhaps I just happened to be at the wrong place and at the wrong time. All in all, we met and that allowed us both to develop a pretext that neither one of us had lived a meaningful life before we were introduced to one another and stepped into this new world.

"Kate, I'm sorry. That was selfish of me to say. I am excited that you're going to have our baby. I just have to try to keep things straight in my head. The bishop concerns me a little. He's going to have to know and I should be the one to tell him. I need to give thought to when and how I will do that. One thing for sure, we certainly welcomed in the New Year with a flair didn't we?"

Matthew passed on the hot chocolate that night and left a little earlier than usual. Johnny Carson bid the world goodnight and I watched, alone. It seemed to have become a habit that once Matthew had returned to the rectory and settled in for the night, he would call. That night, the phone didn't ring.

CHAPTER 26

I didn't sleep much that night. I kept waking up, touching the phone to make certain that it was properly nestled into its cradle. I just wondered why Matthew hadn't called. My head knew why but that reasoning didn't jive with what my heart was feeling at all. I placed my hands on my belly, cuddling the ever so tiny baby whose microscopic-sized heart was already beating right there inside me.

"It's just you and me, Babe!" I said, "It's just going to be the two of us, but we'll be fine." I closed my eyes and fell into another round of sleep.

Morning came early and I was up, showered and off to work. I arrived, parked my car in the usual spot behind the high school and hurried into the building. Greeting teachers along the way, I anxiously made my way to my office and unlocked the door. Moments after stepping foot into my workplace, I experienced my first bout with morning sickness. Being the girls' physical education teacher afforded me the luxury of having a private bathroom in my office. That was a welcomed benefit because my morning visit to the porcelain queen was like clockwork.

That day, my ability to concentrate on my classes was challenged; I was energized and so happy about my baby but concerned about not having Matthew around to share this with. Also, not being able to say anything to anyone just yet was another difficult piece to this puzzle.

The school day had ended, and I was waiting to meet with the student officers of the high school athletic association. My phone rang. I answered. It was Matthew. He never called me at school—what now?

"Hi Kate, I just wanted to apologize for last night. I was in a bit of a daze and just couldn't seem to pull myself together. I'm sorry." I was so happy to hear his voice that I was absolutely forgiving. Never gave it a second thought.

"I, too am sorry, Matthew. I shouldn't have dropped that on you so suddenly. I was just so excited and anxious to share our baby with you that I just couldn't have waited another moment."

"That's okay, Kate, I understand. I am so happy about this baby now that I've had time to think about it. I'll see you tonight; just wanted to make sure that you know how sorry I am for being so self indulging. I love you very much."

"I love you, Matthew, see you tonight." WOW, I thought, WOW! I was so happy to have heard from him. I was thrilled to know that he was elated about the baby. Again, things couldn't be better.

At least I didn't want to believe that things could be better. The reality of it all was still very prominent in my mind. Something was prowling around in my head just waiting to ambush my frame of mind. There would never be three. Deep down in my heart, I knew that there would be but two. Matthew was still a priest. The collision course that we both originally accepted and set out on was a path that we had knowingly chosen. Had this intriguing journey come to an end?

As I sat in the straight-back wooden chair at my desk, my thoughts began to wander. Being pregnant carried with it so many responsibilities and ramifications. If Matthew remained a priest, he would have to walk away from his very own flesh and blood. Would this be the ultimate sacrifice or the blistering alternative? After years of impeccable service, could he nullify his vows to his bishop and leave the priesthood in order to marry? Would the Vatican acknowledge and permit his laicization in order to pay tribute to the woman he loved and child that he created? Would he leave a very comfortable lifestyle with no worries or challenges to face the wilderness of the world? Would he leave a very calm way of life to enter the unknown and sometimes hectic mode of everyday living? Could he place the needs of a child and a wife before his own? Too many no's to these questions---could it be that the reality of it all had been entirely eclipsed by the lust and dangers of this love affair? As much as I loved Matthew with all my heart, I truly believed that Matthew loved Matthew with all of his heart.

As for me, I could handle being a single parent. I would resign from my teaching position. I would be a stay-at-home mom caring for my newborn and for my mother at least for the first few years of my baby's life. Since my dad had left me an inheritance and I had saved a little money, I could do this. My lifestyle would certainly change, and challenges would await me. I would willingly dedicate my life to the fulfillment of the life of my child. It would mean finding and preparing for a new career. My life as I knew it would be history; that was a little adventurous. On the other hand, what if there was a chance that Matthew and I would parent this baby together? The knocking on my office door helped me re-enter the moment. The students had arrived for their scheduled meeting.

Amid all of my students, two of them had become good friends. They were among the group that had arrived. I sometimes found the solitude and privacy that was being demanded of me because of the nature of my relationship very difficult. Just not being able to share the news of my pregnancy or any other thoughts that I was sorting through during this time was challenging. Because I trusted Debbie and Cathy explicitly, the desire had become very powerful to tell them at least about a little of what I was experiencing. I just knew that they would understand, protect and be supportive. I said nothing.

I left school late that afternoon and swung by a local restaurant to pick up takeout for dinner. Mealtime was pleasant as I shared the highlights of my day with my mother. About 9:30 that evening, I heard the hum of Matthew's car pulling into the yard. I could feel a huge smile appear on my face, I was just so happy to see him. I swung open the door and there he stood, with a colossal grin on his face! We embraced, as though we had been apart forever. We melted into one another's arms. It felt so right, it just felt so right. How could this be so wrong then?

It was a wonderful evening. We enjoyed squash soup and a variety of appetizers. We sipped on our stand by, a cup of hot chocolate peaked with the enhancement from the peppermint stick. That had become our night cap. Bette Midler was on with Johnny Carson that night. As usual, we thoroughly enjoyed being together. Nevertheless, there seemed to be a little something different between Matthew and me, almost as though that electrifying chemistry had been short-circuited. Something was wrong— even though the evening appeared to have been so good, we were poles apart. Commonalities had become dissimilar, unidentifiable, unrelated.

CHAPTER 27

My teaching days seemed somewhat mundane because I was so pre-occupied with my life's state of affairs. It had been one week to the day since I had told Matthew of my pregnancy. I was preparing to leave school when my office phone rang. It was Matthew. He said not to prepare any food for us on this particular night. Although his mannerism was kittenish, his voice had that air about it that led me to suspect that he was concealing something – something perhaps that I wouldn't want to hear.

I heard Matthew's car a little after ten o'clock that night, a little later than usual. As he entered the house, he didn't remove his clerical collar. He did hug me, but it felt like a courtesy gesture not an embrace between two people in love. He held me in his arms with no affection, no sincerity. It was sort of like he was playing out expected behavior. The fun and antics were missing in his actions. He didn't have any melody in his voice and certainly no twist of humor to his words.

Uh, oh—what's with the sternness? Matthew's pensive behavior I immediately associated with bad news. Unwilling to stay in limbo any longer, I was curt and to the point when I said, "Okay, let's talk!"

Matthew led the way into the family room, walking slowly with his eyes fixed downward toward the floor. He sat on the rocking chair. I went to the couch. Facing one another, physical distance wasn't the only thing that separated us.

"It's about the baby, Kate…we need to talk more about you having this baby."

"This baby," he had said. "My baby is not *this* baby. What's wrong with him?" I thought.

"I love you, Kate, I love you so very, very much, and I wish I could be happy about your pregnancy, but I can't. You need to understand that in my position, it's just not possible for me to be part of this. It's really not even possible for you to have this baby."

...not possible for you to have this baby...something was very wrong with that statement.

"Wait, wait... let's take this one step at a time," I replied. "I understand that it may not be possible for you to have anything to do with our baby. It's perfectly fine with me, Matthew. If you don't want or can't take on the responsibilities of a child, that's okay. But—what's with the 'it's not possible for you to have this baby' part? That doesn't make any sense to me at all. Exactly what do you mean?"

"What I mean, Kate, is that we can't have this baby together. As a matter of fact, you can't have this baby at all. Think about it—can you imagine what having a baby would do to us or if not to us, to me?"

"Not to us, Matthew not to us. More to you...what would my having this baby do to you?"

"Look, I'm sorry, Kate. I don't want to hurt you but you must understand that we just can't go through with this pregnancy. Here, I'll move over next to you and we'll try to talk through this dilemma together. I hate to see you distressed."

He slowly walked to the couch and sat beside me. He wrapped his arms around me, and I slowly moved away from him. Normally, I would have snuggled up and placed my head on his shoulder being ever so content to just be with him. Not tonight. It was a whole different playing field and the game rules had changed; actually, we no longer were on the same team.

"Why, again, can't I have my baby?" I asked.

"Dear, dear Kate. Just try to relax. We'll talk in a little bit," Matthew responded.

Suddenly I felt captive, like a prisoner in shackles. I pulled even further away from Matthew and looked at him, shaking my head in disagreement.

"I'm not certain that there's a whole lot to talk about right now. I really would like to have some time to myself," I said. "Please, let's call it a night."

Perfect

Respecting my wish and without any further discussion, Matthew said goodnight, kissed my forehead and whispered softly that he would call me tomorrow. I heard the kitchen door close and he was gone. Sabrina never left my side. She knew. The phone didn't ring that night and if it had, I probably would not have answered it.

I twisted and turned and just couldn't get the words "it's not possible for you to have this baby" out of my head. I was wide awake to see the sunrise that morning, but for whatever reason, the beauty that I was privileged to witness just didn't have the impact on me that it had had in the past. I was almost insensitive to my surroundings.

Saturday, nearly noontime, the phone rang.

"Good morning, Kate—Are you feeling better this morning?"

"Not really," I answered in a rather cold voice.

"I'll come a little earlier tonight, like nine or so. How about I bring something for us to eat? We haven't had plain old pizza for a long time; I'll pick one up. Loaded except forget the anchovies, right? Can't go without our hot chocolate though, okay?"

"Fine." And that ended the conversation.

I needed to go someplace where I could be alone to think—and feel. Fortunately, my aunt Julia had called that she was coming to have coffee with mother early that afternoon; that would give me the opportunity to skip out for a little while and try to pull myself back together.

She was true to her word. About one o'clock my aunt arrived. I left shortly thereafter and drove to a favorite spot at a local college that overlooked a small, man-made lake. It was a very tranquil, pretty site, so serene and calm. The air was brisk, refreshing. Within that mini paradise was a large rock that for me was ever so dominating, solid and secure. I loved to climb to the top and sit; and so, I did. It was a little more challenging because there were snowy patches, but I managed. Once atop the boulder I felt safe. Everything was pretty from there, peaceful and solemn. My head overflowing with words frightened me. I could feel my heart filling with pain.

I can't have my baby. That was the all-encompassing remark that Matthew had made to me. My mind was a whirlwind. Nothing made sense. I couldn't understand how he would even think of my not having my baby. What was he thinking? Adoption? Abortion? As a Catholic priest, it certainly wouldn't be thoughts of abortion. Could it be adoption? It would have to be. Catholics believe in the sanctity of life; that life begins at conception—and he's saying that I can't have my baby? What is that all about? I was so lost—I felt like my body had become an item for negotiation and I had lost total control. I had nowhere to turn and no one to talk to. My only friend, my soul mate was the very one who was inflicting this turmoil.

I needed to pull myself together and become strong and take a stand, or I could truly believe that Matthew would never allow anything to happen that would hurt the baby or me. He loved me; when push came to shove, he'd be there for me. I knew it, but could I trust it?

I looked down at my watch. I'd been gone for a little over an hour. I needed to get back, so as not to arouse any suspicion that something was wrong. I carefully slid down the rock, stood erect, took a deep breath of fresh air, walked around the pond, avoiding the many icy spots, and then headed for my car.

I arrived home and had a cup of coffee and a brief visit with my aunt. Although no one knew about my pregnancy, I felt absolutely invaded and totally transparent. It just seemed to me as though my situation was common knowledge and everyone was watching the next step. I cooked dinner for my mother and together we sat at the kitchen table sharing general conversation. I didn't eat.

This was one of the few times that Matthew actually arrived when he said he would (except New Year's Eve when he appeared surprisingly early!). He had pizza in hand and a smile on his face. He was so much better at masking his feelings than I was. Upon his dramatic entrance, he pulled off his collar and tucked his priesthood into his pocket, hugged me ever so tightly as would a man to his wife and pulled me gently as he floated nonchalantly into the family room.

"Paper plates tonight," I said, "Back to basics. No fanfare." Matthew laughed and reached over to give me another hug. For whatever reason, I felt myself pull away. He didn't react to the withdrawal. Sitting across from me Matthew helped himself to the first, second and additional slices of pizza and at no time even suggested that I might join him in this indulgence. This behavior was so far out of character for him. It was obvious that he was on a mission.

"You know, Kate, a cold glass of Pepsi would be good. Do you have any?"

Normally, he would have never had to ask. I would have served him that beverage long before the thought of being thirsty would have even entered his mind. Tonight, things were different.

"Of course—your wish is my command, me lord," I sarcastically answered.

I didn't eat. I just couldn't think of food, not even pizza. Out of sheer politeness, even un-invited, I did cut off a narrow slice and just played with it as I moved it from side to side on my bright white paper plate. Matthew didn't seem to notice. If he did, he never made mention.

All these little acts of alienation went unnoticed. It was almost as though his body was present but his very own heart and mind were not. Sort of like an actor on stage. I had seen that actor perform before. A quick flashback of our trip to Quebec went through my mind. I replayed the moment when, totally without effort, he convinced one of his parishioners that she had mistaken him for her parish priest. Was that what was happening here tonight? Had I fallen in love with a man who had really never existed? Was he suddenly going to unmask and step out of his role?

Something was so wrong, so very wrong. The Matthew that I knew would never have behaved like this. Perhaps the real question should have been: Who is Matthew?

As I sat there staring at him, I felt absolutely nothing. I couldn't get out of my head his comment about my not being able to have my baby; not only did the man I love say this to me, but these words had come from the mouth of a Catholic priest. My head hurt, my stomach hurt and for the very first time ever, I didn't even like Matthew and just couldn't wait for him to leave. Good, bad or indifferent, I was all alone in my own little world until a voice invaded my privacy.

"I've made an appointment for us to see someone for counseling," Matthew just sort of blurted out. "I think that we need to put everything into perspective, and the two of us can't seem to get to that point. I have just the man who can help us, Kate. Although he's extremely busy, he's willing to see us as quickly as tomorrow, after hours though, at 9 p.m. I'll pick you up about 8:45 p.m. and we'll go to his office together. It's close by. His office is right up here on Main Street.

In total disbelief I stumbled through words beginning with: "Going where…for what? I don't quite understand. What is going to see this man all about, Matthew? Counseling you say?"

"Yes, counseling for us, Kate—you need to better understand what having this baby means."

"Well, if it's for us, why are you saying that I need to better understand? Am I the only one involved in this Matthew? Whereabouts were you when all of this happened? And where are you now?"

"That will all be discussed tomorrow and you'll feel much better once we talk with him. Now, do you need to make arrangements for Gretchen to stay with your mother?"

"I'll handle it, thank you. I'll be ready at 8:45. See you then."

Matthew stood up, leaned over, kissed my forehead and then, silently walked away. I spent an unrestful night twisting and turning from side to side desperately trying to piece these pieces together. I felt abandoned, forsaken by the very man with whom I had trespassed into unauthorized territory and had consciously wandered into the sea of immoral pleasures. Was it judgment time? If so, where then was Matthew?

I heard nothing from him until he picked me up the following evening when he drove in the driveway shortly after 7:30. Bidding my mother and Gretchen goodnight, I walked out of the house and over to the car. I opened the door. Matthew had his usual smile and greeted me with a warm and welcoming hello. That very moment was so happy and light that it was almost as though we were heading out to share a long awaited, well planned evening of dining and entertainment! It wasn't so.

CHAPTER 28

It was but a few minutes before we drove into a large parking lot and up to a white trailer. The two stairs into this rather rickety looking structure posing as an office had been freshly swept free of snow; they were the kind made of metal that when unused, could slide under the structure. Inside there were three folding metal chairs and a card table for a desk. This professional office looked rather shady to me, a far cry from the plush rooms with comfortable couches and chairs that are portrayed on television in scenes where counseling sessions are being held. This space was one narrow space. The card table was gray and on it, a rolodex, papers, pen and a telephone.

Upon our arrival, the narrow, very thin door opened and we were greeted by a stately looking gentleman. He was a minister. The chairs were placed in such a fashion that two of them bordered the table and the third was positioned behind. I was graciously offered the chair that was backstage, in that I ended up physically sitting a bit off to the side and in back of Matthew. The location of that spot made it quite easy to keep me removed from the conversation.

Matthew and the minister carried on their business, and never included at me. An occasional nod and smile from this stranger was the extent of my involvement in this counseling session. Their voices were kept low, and although I could hear them, I wasn't putting meaning to any of the words. I was far too busy trying to figure out why I was even there. Suddenly, the minister's voice interrupted my trance as he said, "How are you feeling, dear?" How was I feeling…how was I feeling…out of the clear blue sky he asked me how I was feeling. I couldn't figure out why he asked nor did I really want to answer him. But I did.

J. C. Soucier

"I'm not sure," was my response. "Not sure."

"That's very common, my dear, it is a confusing time," he said. "It will all be resolved soon; the burden will be lifted and you will feel well again."

His words meant nothing to me. I just wanted to go home.

He picked up and dialed the rotary phone. His conversation seemed secretive. He kept his voice low. He jotted something on a second piece of paper. Once he'd hung up the phone, he proceeded to tear the sheet from the pad and hand it to Matthew. Saying nothing, he stood and extended his hand toward me.

"It was nice meeting you. Trust us, everything will be fine," he said as he smiled. I made no move to indicate that I was accepting his assistance to rise from my chair and be escorted to the door. Totally independently, I stood, nodded as I walked past Matthew and the minister and headed toward the door.

Okay, things will be fine, I thought. What exactly did that mean? I didn't know that a whole lot had been left to chance here. I was under the impression that we were coming here for counseling. Had that happened and somehow I had missed it all? Before I knew it, Matthew had taken my arm and walked me to the passenger's side of the car.

Prior to getting in himself, he returned to the trailer and shook the minister's hand, thanking him again. Once in the car he said, "Okay, it's all set, Kate. I have it all right here," as he patted the side pocket of his jacket. "The arrangements are made. We have nothing to worry about. We just need to be there on March 9th at 8 a.m. I'll get the directions and take care of everything. We'll leave the day before, about 9:30 after morning mass and we'll spend a wonderful time in New York. I'll make reservations in the best hotel and we'll eat in the finest restaurant. You wait. You won't be sorry."

"Sorry? Why would I not be sorry? Why would I be sorry? What? Why are we going to New York?" All these questions were shooting out one after another, not waiting for Matthew to respond.

"I'll come over tomorrow night and we'll talk all about it, Kate. Don't worry. I'll take good care of you. I love you and I don't want anything to hurt you."

"Stop—hold it. I just figured this out. You're taking me to New York to have an abortion? What? No—are you out of your mind? No, no New York, no abortion, NO! Let me out, Matthew. Get me home and let me out!" I could hear my voice getting louder and louder, and I didn't care.

Paying absolutely no attention to me, Matthew drove into the driveway, jumped out of the car, ran to my side and opened the door. Before letting me out, he leaned over and kissed me on the cheek. I pulled away from him, ducked under his arm and ran into the house. As I entered, I heard him say, "I'll be here tomorrow."

I walked into the house, still totally bewildered. My mother was sound asleep and Gretchen was reading. I thanked her for her kindness and without further conversation went to my room. Gretchen realized that something was terribly wrong and followed me.

"What's wrong, honey?" she said. "Are you feeling okay?"

I appreciated that someone showed concern and I wanted so badly to bare my soul, but I just couldn't.

"I'll be fine, thank you, Gretchen. I just have a little upset stomach."

"Then you take care of yourself, do you hear? I know, before I leave, I'll make you some hot tea and that will help to calm you and you'll sleep so much better."

I accepted the offer. As I sat in bed, I slowly sipped the tea and tried to pull it all together. I couldn't even think of what had just happened, and neither could I sleep. Holding my belly as though protecting it from being ripped away from me, I cried and cried and cried.

A sudden tap on my arm startled me. I wasn't in my bed at all; the trip from New York was finally over and Matthew's vehicle was in my yard. I turned toward him, still a little bit dazed, only to find a totally blank expression on his face as he said, "You're home. Please get out."

I was hesitant to leave the situation unresolved, yet it was obvious that this is how he wanted to handle it, so I accommodated him. I opened the car door and stepped out. Hearing the trunk pop open, I walked to the back of the car. Normally, Matthew would have had my luggage in hand and would have carried it up the stairs for me. Today, I carried my own suitcase.

As I walked by his door, I looked down expecting that he in return, would at least look up. He didn't. Our eyes never met. I walked up the stairs and into the house as I heard his car pull away. I never looked back.

CHAPTER 29

H ome, finally I'm home, I silently said to myself.

"Hi Mom," I called out. Although my mother and I lived in the same house, she knew nothing of my pregnancy or the fiasco that I'd been through. I couldn't tell her, couldn't tell anyone, so I had to suppress my emotions and pretend. I needed to fabricate a story about this wonderful overnight trip to the Big Apple that I'd just taken with friends, a trip important enough to have taken personal days from school, and the grand time that we'd had. The problem was that I was not a good liar, so the less said the better.

It was my good fortune that when I arrived, my mother happened to be sitting in a room away from the entrance into the house. That gave me the opportunity to freshen up and try to conceal any and all signs of chaos that had overtaken my mental, physical and emotional states.

"Mom, I'll be right in. Let me get my things put away and I'll join you. Don't bother to come out. Shall I bring in some beverage?"

"Nothing for me, dear," she responded, "I'm just anxious to hear about your trip."

"Yikes! She's anxious to hear about my trip," I thought. What will I tell her? I took a little bit of extra time to pull myself together and somehow manage to hide from my mother any telltale sign of the horrendous sequence of events that I had experienced over the last 24 hours. It was a bittersweet time for me. First, I was trying to bounce back from the trauma of not only having been to an abortion clinic, but having been seconds away from taking the very life of my baby whom already I loved so; second, I was attempting to digest the reality of Matthew's intentions and third, I had just made one of the most important decisions I would ever have to make in my lifetime. Now, on top of it all, I needed to have something to say to my mother.

I took twenty or so minutes before appearing in the family room. I'd grabbed a beverage and a yogurt—I was starving. Luckily, just moments after my sitting down, a family friend dropped in to visit; unbeknown to her, she rescued me.

By the time our friend left I was ready for bed. Totally fatigued from the trip and all its details, I helped my mother get into bed and then retired myself. Tired or not, I no longer had reason to stay up and wait. It was 9:30 p.m. Normally, Matthew would arrive about now. Everything was quiet and the lights were all out. Never again would there be the sound of his car, a welcoming hug, the leisurely sharing of evening treats, hot chocolate with a twist of peppermint, watching Johnny Carson—sharing our love. This would never be again.

I turned onto my side, cuddled my belly and thought of the day when I would actually hold my baby in my arms. I closed my eyes and drifted into the beautiful world of tomorrow saying: "It's just you and me, Babe, just you and me – we'll be just fine.

I had the weekend to come to grips with my situation. I needed to think about the future and prepare to move forward with my head held high. Where would I begin and how would I proceed? Many decisions, combined together, would make it all work. So my plan was to begin at the beginning.

A whole new chapter in my life had started. As a child, my grandmother would occasionally remind me that it is a fool who fails to return to the place of her last happiness; strangely enough, circumstances had made that possible. I had come home to the sanctity that my father had built for me. I felt good about being able to work toward putting together a life for my baby and me that would give this child a solid base, perhaps not rich in money but certainly overflowing with love. That would conquer all, I believed. I didn't expect the challenges that would present themselves during the growing period of this precious creation, nor did I anticipate the demons that awaited me.

Perfect

Several weeks went by and not a word from Matthew. I had no idea what was happening with him. It was almost as though we had never existed. I wanted to believe that separating cold turkey was very doable, but that just wasn't the case. I spent many of my evenings feeling very sad, just looking out a window, knowing that I would never again experience the joys associated with the anxieties of waiting for Matthew's arrival. I thought about the many nights that we had spent together; thoughts that now would be memories, treasured memories. These melancholy moments were accompanied by the discomforts of nausea. I just couldn't keep anything down. The combination of vomiting and my inability to handle ending the relationship was a terrible blend. I felt so powerless.

My nights were long. Repeated dashes to the bathroom kept me awake. It was Monday morning and I called the doctor's office concerned that my emotional and physiological state would have adverse effects on my baby. His order was to get to the emergency room immediately. I drove myself. Moments after my arrival, I was checked by a doctor and admitted.

Within a few minutes after I had been taken up to my room, I had a needle in my arm and was hooked to an IV. The liquid was racing through my veins. I felt better already. The vomiting had stopped. Once settled in, the nurse told me that Dr. Robert Martin, my obstetrician, would be in shortly to chat with me. While waiting, I couldn't help but flash back to the experience of having been in an abortion clinic in New York just a few days before. The image of that huge, cold, white room was still so vivid in my mind. The memory of feeling that I was simply part of a process that was wrapped within an uncaring, matter-of-fact, move-along, people-are-waiting-attitude hovered in my mind. How could I ever forget the gut-wrenching emotions that tore me apart?

Being in this hospital was so different. I felt safe, not threatened. I had all the confidence in the world in my doctor; I just knew that my baby and I were in the best of hands. That mattered, it mattered so much.

Moments later, a dark-haired man wearing a white lab coat walked into my room.

J. C. Soucier

"Good morning, Kate," he said as he pulled a chair close to my bedside. "How are you feeling?"

"Much better now, Dr. Martin," I replied, "I've had a couple of pretty rough weeks."

"You have?" he replied. "And what's happened in these couple of rough weeks?"

It was at that time that I told Dr. Martin all about my experience. It took so long—at least it felt that way. He never for a moment hurried me. I cried. I sobbed. It was just so difficult. Thinking about what had transpired in New York was one thing, but to actually tell someone how close I had come to losing my baby was near impossible. Before this, no one knew.

"I'm so sorry for your suffering, and I certainly don't want to add more, but... there is more. Perhaps giving birth to this baby is not what God wants of you right now, Kate; since He is the Keeper of the Stars then what He chooses, goes. It looks as though you are going to deliver prematurely, Kate. You'll lose the baby within the next twenty-four hours. I am so sorry, dear."

"I can't lose this baby, Dr. Martin. What needs to happen for me to keep this pregnancy? What do I need to do?" I said, begging for a solution.

"There's nothing more that can be done, Kate. Your test results show that the process of having a spontaneous abortion has already started. Falling short of a miracle, there's absolutely nothing that anyone can do. We now need to focus on your health, Kate. I am putting you on complete bed rest. Listen to me carefully. You may not get up for any reason, including bathroom privileges. We're pumping fluids into you as fast as your body will accept them; there's always room for a wonder, but that's our last hope, dear. Other than that, there's absolutely nothing that can be done. I so wish there were. It's in God's hands now, Kate."

"God wants my baby to make it. He gave me the strength to protect his life once before, and He will do it again." I just knew deep down in my heart that God wanted this baby to be born as much as I did. He had handpicked a place for both of us on this earth along with a purpose, and I wasn't about to give up now.

"We'll make it, Dr. Martin, watch and see. We'll make it," I said.

Perfect

Nodding his head as though he really believed in what I was saying, Dr. Martin clasped my hand between both of his, looked directly into my eyes and said, "Try to rest, Kate—it's what can help the most right now. I'll be back this afternoon. Keep the faith, girl. For whatever reason, you sound pretty convinced and convincing. You just might see that mission through to the end." Then he walked out the door.

Tears began to run slowly down my cheeks as I looked out the window and across the street. There was the high school football field that was covered with snow. Everything was white. I gently placed my hands on my belly and could feel the warmth that I was generating.

Be safe, Little One, I whispered, nothing will harm you. Together we can be strong, and we'll make it. Just don't let go, don't let go—and neither will I.

I had to stop crying. Storing up every ounce of energy was essential right now, and crying took a physical and emotional toll on my body. I realized that. I dried my tears and positioned myself in this not very soft hospital bed. I leaned into the multiple pillows that the nurse had kindly brought to me and sipped the seltzer water that was on the rolling table.

Feeling confident that God would give me the privilege of carrying my baby to term, I closed my eyes and allowed myself the luxury of floating into a field of images, beautiful images, fantasizing about my baby—sex, hair color, eye color, smile. He's a boy, I thought. The feeling of his sex was so strong that it was actually more awareness than a feeling. Totally wrapped up in the beauty of the baby growing within, I never gave another thought to the possibilities of losing him. I simply continued to dream.

Suddenly, and much to my dismay, this as clear as life panorama of handsome images was interrupted abruptly.

"Kate?"

I recognized the voice. It was not who I wanted to see.

CHAPTER 30

There he was. Matthew was walking into my hospital room. With a hint of a smile on his face, he approached my bed. He leaned over to kiss my forehead and I turned away from him. He didn't make an issue of my having dodged his attempt; he simply kissed me on the cheek, pulled a chair to my bedside and sat down.

In an ever so soft voice he said, "I've been so worried about you. When I heard that you had been admitted into the hospital I couldn't wait to get here. I'm so sorry for the way I treated you, Kate. It was selfish and very insensitive of me. I realize now how much you want this baby. I am so, so sorry." His hand touched my shoulder.

"Losing the baby after such a struggle must be so difficult for you—it should not be ending this way. I wish I could help, Kate. I'm told that everything that can be done medically has been done, but you just couldn't beat the odds. I feel just terrible."

I didn't look up, didn't acknowledge his presence, and didn't react. Not only couldn't I believe the words that Matthew was trying so hard to make sound palatable, but I was finding it difficult to accept that he had actually walked into my hospital room after everything that had happened between us. He made no reference to what had happened; no apologies. He focused on what he thought was my baby's destiny and his salvation. And he did all of this sitting very comfortably at my bedside! I was beside myself and couldn't even respond.

He's really convinced that I'm going to lose this baby, I thought, and that's why he's in here. His visit, compounded by his poor choice of words, became the slingshot with which I would slay the dragon. That combination catapulted me over the barrier that had been so difficult to hurdle. This experience was all that I needed to bring me out of the trauma of losing Matthew; my baby and I were now free to move forward.

My strength was at full power. It was as though my body had suddenly been filled with a surge of energy, nurturing this new life within me. I was carrying the future and I was ever so determined to bring that baby to term.

I turned toward Matthew and looked into his ocean blue eyes. Although his face looked gentle and kind, our love as it had been, was history. In a very calm voice I said to him, "Thank you for your visit, Matthew. The baby and I will be fine, so there's really no need for you to come back or ever worry. I love you, always will and so will your child. Go now; return to your protected environment and leave my baby to me to share tomorrow."

Totally speechless and appearing stunned at my assertive reaction to him, Matthew slowly stood up, placed his hand on my head and stroked my hair as he whispered, "I wish things could have been different, Kate. I love you and always will."

He turned and headed for the door. Just before he walked out, he turned and looked at me. I smiled; he smiled. I knew deep down in my heart that the dragon that I would forever love had been slain.

CHAPTER 31

I was discharged from the hospital three days later—very pregnant. Dr. Martin was at my side as the nurse wheeled me to the hospital entrance. From there, I would walk to my car and drive myself home.

"You're carrying a miracle baby, Kate. God certainly has the two of you in the palm of His hand. How wonderful for you. Remember to take it easy and call my office tomorrow to schedule weekly appointments with me just to monitor that little tyke, ok? Take care."

"Thank you, Dr. Martin. We'll be fine, and I will see you religiously every week." Strange choice of words I remember thinking.

When I returned home my mother was anxiously awaiting my arrival. She was so relieved to see that I had recovered quickly and was on the mend from what she believed was a bout with the flu complicated by severe hydration. Where she got that diagnosis one will never know, but, that was her explanation for my brief hospital stay and I did not correct her.

I waited until the following Monday to return to school where I began leading a very normal, happy life. Debbie and Cathy, the students who were good friends of mine hovered over me as though they knew that something was going on. Matthew was out of the picture and although I could forgive him and did, forgetting him would probably really never happen. What really mattered to me were memories of the good times. I had lost my love of life and Matthew had given that back to me. He was and would remain forever my one and only true love, my soul mate and, of course, my baby's father. That would ever change.

I was feeling terrific. Besides teaching, I continued being active coaching and judging women's gymnastics, playing volleyball on a women's league, playing badminton regularly and fencing competitively. The baby was growing daily and I began to feel movement. Nothing was more exciting than to have this little person that was growing inside me, kick or punch me—the wonder of life was such a miracle!

One afternoon, the kitchen door swung open and through it came flying a body that I never expected to see. It was my cousin, Jeanne whom I hadn't seen nor spoken to since the incidence involving her husband.

Jeanne had discovered that her husband, Bob, the very man who was the pillar of the Church, the same man who reported Matthew and me to the bishop for having an affair, was himself being unfaithful to his wife—and had been for years! Overcome by uncontrollable tears, she found her way to me, knowing only too well that she would find a compassionate ear and comfort.

We talked for hours. It was as though our after school visits had never been interrupted. The closeness of our relationship allowed this separation to be mended without an explanation. We proceeded to catch up and did with the exception of my revealing being three months pregnant. Highlights of Jeanne's visit included hearing that Matthew was stopping into her home again. From what she said, Matthew never addressed Bob with the issue of his having run to the chancery about us. Everything simply went on as though nothing had transpired. I was somewhat confused as to how something this life altering could go unspoken; it was beyond me. I couldn't help but wonder if this was just another stage on which Matthew was performing.

The real big news was that at the end of May, Matthew was being transferred to another parish. Word had it that his new congregation was in a community that was located only seventeen miles west of his present location. The best information was yet to come. He was being elevated from secular parish priest to pastor. Since Jeanne knew nothing about my pregnancy, I couldn't respond to the news as I would have liked. I bit my lip. In a somewhat liberating fashion, I just couldn't help but wonder if Matthew was being compensated for staying in the priesthood. Was this a trade-off for turning his back on the responsibilities that come with fathering a child? Would the Church really reward a man who preaches from the pulpit her teachings about the value of family life and then climbs down from the stage and defies those very principles? One will never know the answers to those questions.

We continued drinking coffee and chatting. Jeanne spoke about how she had discovered that Bob had been involved with several other women. She displayed many of the emotions that go along with having been jilted, verbally abused and emotionally injured. After hours of freeing her soul, Jeanne had cleared her mind, unburdened her heart, and now could see how far more beneficial it would be for her and the children if he were to leave the family unit. That was his plan; and little did he know that this would not be a compromising situation for his wife. In the long run, his departure would be a blessing.

As Jeanne was ready to leave, I walked her to the door where we said our goodbyes. She appeared to feel much better from when she first arrived. She looked relieved, energized and ready to take on the situation that awaited her.

What a great day this has been for both of us, I thought. Jeanne's findings would free her from years of misery and would give her children fresh air to breathe. For me, being reunited with my best friend was such a delight.

The timing to have Jeanne back in my life couldn't have been better. She would come to my home for coffee and that would be special. It would be like old times all over again. Well, maybe not quite like old times.

CHAPTER 32

Early one Saturday morning the telephone rang. I picked it up, said hello and heard the following:

"Hello Kate, this is Eloise, Matthew's sister."

"Well, good morning, Eloise. What a surprise to hear your voice."

"I hope I'm not disturbing you; I'm coming into Lewiston a little later today and thought that we might get together for a mid-afternoon lunch. Would you meet with me, Kate?"

"Sure, Eloise," I answered. "Getting together sounds like a fun idea. Where were you thinking of meeting?"

"How about at Happy Jack's about two o'clock?"

"Happy Jack's at two o'clock it is. See you there."

I hung up, but was somewhat puzzled over this call and the invitation. Eloise was a person whom I had probably seen three or four times. Always at Jeanne's, always amidst a crowd that had gathered to celebrate one thing or another. To have her call me out of the clear blue and invite me out to a mid-afternoon lunch was very much out of the ordinary. I wasn't totally comfortable with the whole idea--didn't know why, just found the invitation odd.

I joined my mother at the kitchen table for a cup of tea. I didn't tell her about the call from Eloise, but I just couldn't get it out of my mind. With errands to run, I finished my tea and was off to accomplish what I had planned to do. Time seemed to fly by and before I knew it, it was 1:45 p.m. I headed for the restaurant.

I entered, and within moments, Eloise was at my side and escorting me to the table that she had chosen. It was in a corner, a far corner at that. Strange choice, I thought, especially since there were so many other locations with empty tables to choose from.

We sat across from each other and started our conversation

with general pleasantries. The waiter presented us with a menu and requested our beverage of choice. Returning immediately with two glasses of water, he took our order and left. Moments following, Eloise, in a very assertive voice said, "I know that you're pregnant, Kate, and that my brother is the father."

"Excuse me? Exactly what are you saying and where did you get this information?" I answered.

"Don't play games with me," she said. "Matthew tells me everything we're very close you know. Now, Kate, tell me, is this true?"

"I suggest you go back to your brother, Eloise, and ask him since you're so close."

"Well, you know that we can't let this happen, right? It will ruin my brother."

"Ruin your brother? Ruin your brother? Excuse me, Eloise, exactly what is it that you're saying?

"I'm saying that you don't have a choice. This isn't about you here. You must have an abortion."

"I must have an abortion? If in fact I am pregnant, Eloise, carrying a human life that is a kicking, punching, breathing baby who is my flesh and blood and is Matthew's future as well as mine, what right would you have to dictate my plans? I would already love this baby with all my heart and you're suggesting that I abort? Go talk to your brother, Eloise; we have nothing further to discuss."

As I began to rise from my chair, Eloise blurted into a monologue saying: "You're being a selfish bitch, Kate. You never loved my brother. By having this baby, you'll ruin him and that's all you want to do, isn't it? Well, you can't do it. You have no choice. I won't let you and if you don't listen to me, you'll have to listen to the Church. They won't let you get away with this. I will give you the money for the abortion. I'll make all the arrangements and I'll even drive you."

At that point I really needed to leave. I was so ready to unleash words that would have bordered verbal abuse that I got up and walked away. A feeling of strength surged through my body as I swung open the restaurant door.

Perfect

Yes! And a second dragon bites the dust! I said to myself with conviction as I walked toward my car.

Before returning home, I looped around to sit by my favorite pond and have a little time to cry over this encounter. The intensity of this meeting had caught up with me and I needed to collect my thoughts. That was a heart-wrenching conversation that I had with this woman, and I needed to rid myself of that poison. Once out of my system, I felt together enough to head home. The last thing I wanted was to give my mother reason to be concerned about my well-being.

A little time engulfed by the beauty of nature and I was ready to meet the world.

CHAPTER 33

T he school year had come to an end and facing my last day was sad. I was leaving behind a lot of history. I had been a student there myself and then had returned fresh out of college as a teacher for the next seven years. It was too soon to say anything to anyone, and I felt terrible not being able to at least tell Debbie and Cathy. I just could not do that, so I didn't. I had been bringing home personal belongings from my office so that on the last day, when I closed my office door behind me for the last time, there would be no residue of my ever having been there. I took one final look at the gym where for the past seven years I had spent so much of my time. I closed the door and walked away. A tear dropped onto my cheek as I realized that this very happy chapter of my life had ended..

I was still going for my weekly prenatal visits, and Dr. Martin had given an October 5 due date. Each day, my baby was growing. Each day, I thanked God for allowing me to carry and give life to this precious little person. My bump was barely noticeable; however, I just knew that I would awake one morning and there it would be. Now that school had ended, I was free to be pregnant publicly and I couldn't wait for this little guy to show himself!

My letter of resignation had been written, and my plan was to mail it immediately after making the announcement of my pregnancy to my family. Originally, I was going to tell my mother first and then my Aunt Julia and Jeanne. A second thought was to tell the three of them together. That way, it would be done in one swoop and they would all hear the same words at the same time, giving less room for any misunderstanding and, if needed, they had one another for moral support.

I called my Aunt and cousin to invite them for coffee and dessert. I also put a bug in their ear that I had a little something to share with them. They arrived shortly after lunch and I was ready. My mother, aware that they were joining us, was looking forward to their visit and greeted them with her natural warmth.

As everyone sat around the table enjoying their coffee and dessert, exuberant and not able to wait another minute, I made the grand announcement.

"I'm pregnant and the baby is due October 5," were my words, not offering any additional information. Nothing was said about the identity of the baby's father and no questions were asked. My unspoken words made the message very clear.

All three accepted the news very well. My mother said she suspected my pregnancy.

"I've been feeling a bit of a bump in your belly when you lean against me to wash my hair," she said. "Actually, I'm looking forward to the day when I can feel the baby move or kick!" Little did she know that the baby had been moving around quite actively but he must have just been napping at times when such movement would have confirmed my mother's suspicion of my pregnancy. Thankfully, his timing was perfect!

My aunt said, "I wonder if he'll be a little red head." Guess it's difficult to keep secrets from neighbors.

Jeanne smiled and jumped up from her chair, came over to me and hugged me as she exclaimed, "Congratulations! I am so happy for you!"

The initial presentation of the news went very well. Now I could mail my letter to the superintendent of schools and look to the future. From this point on, it wasn't important to me who knew, who told who whatever. The one thing that would remain tightly locked away in my heart was the identity of my baby's father. Matthew's name would not be spoken from my lips—not until the day arrived when his own child would ask to meet his father. I was comfortable with that arrangement.

A few days passed and Debbie and Cathy knocked at my door. They were frequent visitors and dropping in unannounced was not unusual and very welcomed. Now was the time to tell them. And so, I did. Taken totally by surprise, they were upset with me that I would not be returning to school but then overjoyed because they saw how radiant and jubilant I was. Having told them was a huge and long overdue effort.

Summer was in full bloom. I was happy, healthy and feeling wonderful. Every day I would go out to my little garden in the backyard to watch the growth of my labor. Walking up and down the narrow rows of dirt and just being among nature's gifts made me feel fulfilled. I enjoyed every minute of it. Once the vegetables started to grow, I would harvest the crop and proudly bring it in to my mother. Her smile and gratefulness always gave me a feeling of accomplishment.

Every evening, we would sit out on the deck enjoying the fresh summer air and playing Scrabble or reading. I would read to my baby and my mother would simply sit quietly and listen. On this particular evening the phone rang.

"Hello," I answered.

"Yes, hello. May I speak to Kate, please?"

"This is."

"Kate, this is Father DeVille. I'm calling on behalf of Father Matthew; I'm really calling about Father Matthew. Would you please meet with me? I have something very important to discuss with you."

"Er….Father DeVille—I'm sorry, why would I want to meet with you?"

"I have something very important to discuss with you. It concerns Father Matthew."

"All right, when and where would you like to meet, Father DeVille?"

"I would appreciate it if you would come to St. Paul's Retreat Center in Augusta, maybe as soon as Thursday evening. Could you do that, Kate?"

"Where is St. Paul's Center, Father? I'm really not familiar with Augusta." He went on to give me directions.

"Is seven o'clock a convenient time for you, Kate?"

"I'll be there at seven on Thursday, Father."

"Thank you, Kate. I'll see you then." And he hung up.

"Here we go again," I thought. Maybe there was something to

J. C. Soucier

Eloise's statement that made reference to the Church not allowing me to have my baby. Actually, "What could they really do now?" was my thought. I wasn't intimidated by Father DeVille's call, but I was puzzled, perplexed and perhaps a little curious. Exactly what could they be thinking?

I discussed this with my mother and she had good advice.

"Just relax, Kate. Second guessing them will just upset you, and their actual ideas won't surface until you meet with this priest tomorrow night. So...read on, let's continue to entertain my grandchild."

CHAPTER 34

It was Thursday morning and all was well. I had spent a restless night, concerned over what might be lurking in the shadows, just waiting to pounce on me. Something had caught the attention of the hierarchy of the Catholic Church. Having inquired about Father DeVille, I discovered that he was the Vicar for Religious, like a shepherd managing a flock made up of secular priests. If any of them had problems, they would come to Father DeVille. As I saw it, his role was that of counselor, advocate and parent. So, to meet with Father DeVille was to meet with Matthew's guardian. Did this mean that I would be confronted once again with someone whose mission was to protect a fallen priest?

With a plump little belly, I wouldn't try to conceal my pregnancy nor did I want to flaunt it. I would go to this meeting being simply me. By the same token, I would return home in the same fashion. No threats would frighten me, and no life-altering arrangements would be made. I was ready and so was my canine partner.

Augusta was some thirty-two miles north of Lewiston. The heavens had opened up and it was pouring rain. I estimated that leaving at six o'clock would give me time to drive cautiously, find the location and have a few minutes to spare. I took my raincoat out of the closet, leaned over and patted my husky companion, Sabrina, signaling her to follow. I bid my mother goodnight and began to walk toward the door.

"Drive carefully, Kate," said my mother. "I'll wait up for you."

"Okay, Mom, say a little prayer. I can use all the help I can get. I'm getting up front and center with the big guns tonight." She laughed and nodded. Sabrina and I headed for the garage. I opened the car door, the dog jumped into the front seat of the car and I fol-

J. C. Soucier

lowed her.

I took the interstate as opposed to the back road, making the drive between the two cities that much easier. Once in Augusta, the directions that Father DeVille had given me were very clear. I made it to St. Paul's Retreat Center with fifteen minutes to spare. My thoughts wandered back to the evening when I had dropped Matthew off at the airport prior to his flight to Rome. We had time to spare then…and found a mighty nice way of spending those extra moments. Guess that wouldn't happen tonight.

Sabrina could sense my apprehensiveness. I was not frightened of what awaited me, but I was annoyed, fatigued at the relentless efforts to make me feel guilty that were being pushed at me. In my dog's attempt to comfort me, she nestled under my arm. Her unconditional love and loyalty gave me a sense of security. Unbeknown to either of us, she gave me strength to meet the demon that awaited me.

I almost imposed my desire to bring her in with me, but realized that being a Siberian husky, it was in her nature to protect me, and therefore, if she sensed any threat to me, she could easily become aggressive toward Father DeVille. That behavior would not be in anyone's best interest. Sabrina stayed in my car and I stepped out into the pouring rain, umbrella in hand.

I had been fortunate to find a parking spot on the side of the road directly in front of the very large and stately building. I walked up the front stairs, climbed them to the oversized front door and rang the doorbell. A young seminarian opened the door. He was very courteous as he invited me in, offering to take my coat and umbrella. I gave him my umbrella, which he left opened and placed on the alcove floor. I kept my coat wrapped securely around me.

"Are you here to see Father DeVille?" he asked.

I nodded.

"Please follow me. I'll let Father know that you're here, and he'll join you shortly."

"Thank you," I responded as I smiled and walked into the room that had been designated for our meeting.

The inside of this building was huge and stifling. Marble floors, marble staircase, stoic paintings of religious leaders placed in a very calculated manner, and what appeared to be a multitude of tiny rooms along the long hallway. The room that I entered was perhaps ten feet square. The walls were grayish white and the only artifacts of color were two photos. One of His Holiness and one of the bishop. There were but two wooden chairs and a small mission style table in the stark room, certainly not decorated to radiate warmth. I felt myself become extremely uncomfortable as the door closed behind me and I was left alone in this cold, intimidating space.

Dear God, I prayed, I know that this is a little conflicting in nature because I'm sitting in a building belonging to your direct sales force, waiting to meet with a member who is at the top of the chain in this diocese, but please help get me through this. I don't want to fight; and I can't fight this demon (pardon the inappropriate word) alone—please, give me the strength that I will need to counteract whatever awaits me. Please… and I was interrupted by the opening of the door.

"Kate," he said dominantly, as he extended his hand to shake mine. "I'm Father DeVille. Shall I take your coat?"

"Thank you, I'm fine." I took it off and draped it over the back of my chair. Father invited me to sit down. I did. He didn't.

"How was your drive up? I see we're having our share of rain today."

"My drive was fine, Father," sounding as confident as an Etruscan warrior on a battlefield.

"I had your safety in my prayers and will pray for your safe return. But now, let's get down to business."

How sweet were those words? "He certainly has an agenda and here goes, were my thoughts.

"Kate, I apologize for this short notice, but I asked you to meet with me so soon because time is of the essence. Your pregnancy is, of course, the issue at hand. I met with Father Matthew and he is sick over this. So sick that he's had to take time away from his parish duties."

"Really? I'm sorry to hear that. I certainly would never want anything to happen to Matthew. What does my being pregnant have to do with all of this?"

"It has everything to do with it. Do you have any idea, any idea at all what having this baby and raising it locally will do to this very much loved priest and his reputation? And, do you know how deeply such knowledge among parishioners will scar the name of the Church?"

"I'm sorry, Father, but what is first and foremost in my mind is not protecting Matthew. That's your job and I appreciate your efforts. But, I'm all about protecting my baby."

"Kate you're being totally obstinate. You must understand that you cannot have this child in Maine. You cannot keep this child. As a Catholic your first obligation is to the Church. Having this baby will not only destroy a priest but again, I remind you that you will disfigure the name of the Church. Intentionally you will be doing this. Can you go forth into your future with that on your conscience?"

"Father—in all due respect, my answer to your question is absolutely yes I can. I can and will go forth into the future because I'm doing nothing wrong. I am not destroying Matthew. I am not smearing the name of the Catholic Church. I am simply going to have my baby and we'll live our lives privately with every intention of protecting the good name of his father. To date, the only person to whom I've revealed Matthew's identity is my obstetrician. That was a medical necessity. Now besides those of you within the Church who know, Matthew has told his sister. I'm not asking you to reveal any conversation that you've had with Matthew, but if you've not yet been privy to Eloise's attempt to convince me to have an abortion, you might inquire. Oh, and there is another---perhaps you should ask Matthew about the other, unless of course, you already know."

"We're getting off the track here, Kate. We need to discuss the need for you to have this baby adopted. We will make all the arrangements for you to give birth out of state and come home, leaving your baby behind. The adoption papers will be prepared. You'll have all your accommodations and hospital paid for as well as your travel. This way, everybody comes out a winner and you can begin all over again. You will be totally free. Having a baby to care for would rob you of your freedom, Kate. This way, you will be liberated to lead your life without charge."

"Free? Everybody comes out a winner? Everybody comes out a winner except my baby, Father. Having my baby adopted will liberate my life? Relieve me of being charged with the responsibility of another human being? NO! The answer is no. I want to be charged with the responsibility of this baby. This is my child. How much longer do we need to belabor this point? I will not change my mind. Now, I really would appreciate being left alone."

"Kate, I'm sorry to see that you are being so uncooperative. You obviously have no idea how wonderful adoption can be. There are parents out there who would do anything to have a child. You are robbing a couple of this opportunity. You really don't know anything about adoption, do you?"

"And you really don't know anything about me do you Father? Tell me, is your information about adoption from what you've read in textbooks or have people shared their stories with you? You certainly seem to know so much."

"I do, Kate. I know a lot about adoption, mostly from families who have adopted; they are so happy. The children thrive. As a single parent you will be depriving this child of a good family, of all the opportunities that life will have to offer. Chances are you'll never be able to have a well-paying job because your reputation will be ruined. So how do you expect to provide properly for this baby? You're also putting out there a child that will be a bastard and will be branded. You're thinking only of yourself, and you're willing to let this innocent little baby pay for your mistake. You are going to rob this child of everything life has to offer. If you gave it up, you would be doing the most unselfish act a mother could ever perform. The child would be adopted by a well-established family who could offer him every positive experience and opportunity that life has to offer. He could be an educated and well-adjusted human being. With a single mother, you'll be lucky if he graduates from high school. You have nothing to give this baby, Kate. Let him go."

"You know, Father. Maybe you're right. I probably will never have the luxury of giving my child everything money can buy, but

I truly believe that I can give him a whole lot of what money can't buy. I will dedicate my life to the betterment of his. That will get him to the top."

"You are fantasizing, Kate. How far do you think this child will get?"

"The sky will be his limit, Father, I'll teach him to dream and to believe that his dreams can come true. I hope you stick around and watch." I began to rise and reach for the coat on the back of my chair.

"Before you leave, Kate, I can't stress enough how very idealistic you are being and how destructive that will be for so many people and the Church. You just don't seem to understand the consequences of having and keeping this baby."

"Maybe I don't understand what having my baby means Father, but then, there are many things that I don't understand that are attached to church related experiences that I've had since being pregnant. I can live with all that I've done, can you? Can Matthew? Can you?" I stepped away from my chair, took my coat from the back of the chair, swirled it around and put it on. Father DeVille didn't move nor did he speak. As I opened the door I turned to him and said, "I'll see myself out, thank you. By the way, please don't forget to pray for my safe trip home."

Fortunately the path to the door was a straight line. Upon leaving, I leaned over, picked up my umbrella and stepped out into a very dark, rainy night.

Once in my vehicle, Sabrina was all over me. She knew that I was exhausted from this confrontation and her genuine compassion and love was very healing to me. I locked the doors, started the engine and turned on the defroster. I felt really beaten up. Hugging my dog with both arms, I just broke down and cried.

Was I really such a terrible person? Am I being selfish? Will I deny my baby a good life? Question after question and my answers were all in direct opposition to what I had just heard. Although I cried all the way home, the tears were part of a purging process, a clearing of all doubts that gave my heart permission to be true to my commitment to the wellbeing of my baby which would remain a lifelong dedication.

Perfect

Before I realized it, I was driving into my garage. I walked into the house, Sabrina at my side, and I never got beyond the first chair at the kitchen table. My mother had suspected that I'd been engaged in an emotional battle and she was ready and waiting to pour me a cup of hot chocolate. She knew what a soothing effect that warm, sweet liquid had on me. It had forever been a lifesaver. It actually all began when I was a child and my grandmother and I would sip on hot chocolate every night before bed. I would be sitting in my bed, she beside me as I listened attentively to the stories she would tell in French. The hot chocolate had also worked wonders for Matthew and me, and there was no question in my mind that it would be magical now. With Sabrina sitting beside me and my mother across the table, I relaxed as I enjoyed the calming essence of my very favorite drink. Just being in the comfort of the home that as a child had always provided me with security was also a tranquilizing factor.

After a few minutes of soaking in the influence of this reassuring space, I began sharing with my mother some bits and pieces about my meeting with Father DeVille. I reserved some of the information in fear that it would upset her. Although she was strong in her own rights, she was aging and extremely sensitive to my feelings. After we had chatted, both of us were ready for bed. It had been a trying day for me and an even more taxing evening.

As I lay in bed mulling over yet another experience , I couldn't help but wonder how Matthew had been treated when he was called to the bishop's office in response to Bob's telltale run to the chancery. Being an outsider, with no binding commitment to the Church, I had been verbally raped by a member of the diocesan hierarchy, made to feel like a sinner and a most horrible person. Matthew had made a promise, a promise to obey his bishop, and had broken it. My encounters with the management of disciplinary action by the Church were abusive; I could only imagine that stronger measures were followed when dealing with their own. If that in fact was the case, then I supposed just accepting the consequences for his actions was, by the most part, much easier for Matthew than fighting the system. Apparently, the sympathetic, understanding ear of the Catholic Church seemed to be a missing

J. C. Soucier

piece for us, at least with the keeper of the keys of this diocese.

As I think back to when we were together, Matthew most usually avoided confrontation by patronizing the source. When he arrived to be with me, his behavior was indicative of where he had been and with whom he had spoken, because he truly did live two separate lives. There were times when it seemed like the transition from cleric to lay was more difficult for him, especially during our second attempt at making our relationship work. Those labors became more identifiable. I could tell if he had been in contact with the hierarchy of the Church or with his best priest friend. His demeanor, expressions, style, and social graces were telltales.

If he had been among leaders of the church, his submissiveness was loud. He displayed minimal authority and leadership. His decision-making ability suddenly was non-existent. My suggestions became decisions. On the other hand, his personality was totally different if he had connected with his artist, self-indulging priest friend. This man had a pompous, holier than thou, attitude and paramount behavior that parroted that of a sovereign master. Matthew performed on that stage, acting the more traditional role once associated with priests, that being of supremacy and authority. Both performances were sterling, but then the true, bona fide Father Matthew was neither of them. He was a sensitive, gentle, humorous, adventurous man, who was concerned about the wellbeing of others, a genuine lover of life. That is the man that when with me, walked away from these pseudo characters and into being just plain Matthew. Because I loved him so, I was willing to partake in this Jekyll and Hyde lifestyle.

CHAPTER 35

It was a beautiful summer. A little warm for a very pregnant lady, but in spite of it all, the days were gratifying. The power, the wonder, the energy of a little person growing inside me just made every bead of perspiration well worth it. I enjoyed my daily walks into my little garden. I would breathe the fresh aroma of Mother Nature's many gifts. I also meditated frequently in that little patch of heaven. I talked to my baby often. There were also blocks of time when I would cry, never knowing why; I just did.

I was counting the days before I would finally meet and cuddle ever so tightly in my arms, the most important person in my life. I had decided that my baby, who already held the upper hand, was a boy. I just knew it. As for a name, many had come to mind but none of them were right—it had to be more than a nice sounding name, it had to have meaning—a very attached, unique meaning—because my son's name would be my first and very special gift to him. I was confident that the chosen name would come to me; some way, somehow it would make itself known.

I had subscribed to *Parents Magazine*. I was browsing through the newest publication when the telephone rang.

"Hello," I answered.

"Hello, Kate?"

"Yes."

"Kate, this is Father DeVille. How are you?"

"Father DeVille? Interesting…and, I'm fine, thank you."

"I'm sure that I am not a favorite person to you, Kate, but I have something very important that I need to talk to you about. I must see you as soon as possible."

"Important? What could be so important, Father? I thought we pretty much covered the important stuff when we met a few weeks ago."

"I'd rather not go into details over the phone. This matter is extremely confidential. Please trust me."

In a calm voice I responded, "And when would you like this meeting to take place?"

"Tonight, Kate, it's that urgent."

"Tonight. Where shall we meet tonight?"

"At my rectory in Portland." He went on to give me the address. "The driveway is to the left of the rectory and you will enter from the side door."

"And the time, Father?"

"Would 6:30 be convenient for you?"

Would 6:30 be convenient for me; as though accommodating me was important. "Convenient? I'll be there at 6:30 and I'll use the side entrance. I'll be there," I reiterated and then hung up.

"You look annoyed, Kate, is everything alright?" asked my mother.

"Would you believe that Father DeVille just called—the priest that I met with at St. Paul's Retreat Center not so long ago? He's the very same man who tried to convince me that I should give my baby up for adoption. Remember?"

"How could I not remember, dear? That was a nasty experience for you."

"Well, he wants to meet with me over an extremely confidential matter. So secretive that he chose not to even reference it over the phone. Suppose the rectory phone is bugged—he knows it, of course, and knows what to say and what not to say. Mind you, recording a conversation is only good when it benefits the recorder. Sorry, mother, I don't mean to be so blatant."

"Blatant nothing, Kate, you've taken a whole lot from the Church. I wonder sometimes if they realize how lucky they are that they're dealing with you. I'm thinking that if someone else were in your shoes, the going might not be as smooth for them. Did you agree to meet with him?"

"I did, at 6:30 tonight, at his rectory in Portland."

"Are you sure you want to subject yourself to this again? Or are you simply a glutton for punishment? And, Kate, why didn't he come here or to one of the many rectories in Lewiston? Why is it you who has to travel to accommodate his wish?"

Wow! I had never seen nor heard my mother react to anything like this before. Perhaps she had watched me cry one time too many. I had not thought to reverse the ownership of this encounter, being on one's familiar turf does enhance the security factor I suppose. Oh well, I wasn't particularly concerned about safety and back up, I had made a commitment and nothing--no one--was going to change my decision.

A glass of ice tea was refreshing as we both sat on the deck in silence. I couldn't help but think of my mother's attitude to all of this. Her snappy comeback was so out of character for her. She had really never come to my rescue before. Still waters run deep, and apparently when they overflow, they respect no boundaries. Go Mom!

The grandfather clock struck five o'clock, and its rich sound traveled out onto the deck. That was my cue. I jumped into the shower, changed my clothes, and Sabrina and I were headed to what the next saga had in store. It wasn't raining on this particular evening; actually it was rather peaceful and pretty. I drove to I-95, put my vehicle on cruise and headed down the pike. My thoughts wandered to my last encounter with this very same priest. It was a bit of a disaster, but tonight I was feeling somewhat arrogant and confident. Perhaps my mother's performance earlier that afternoon sparked a little warrior-like attitude in me. Nevertheless, I was ready.

It had to be about Matthew. Father DeVille was going to lunge forth with another attempt, another plea for the salvation of this fallen priest. Stop at nothing to protect him must be the battle cry. Man, don't they ever know when to quit?

Sabrina sensed that although not frightened, I was a little anxious about this meeting. She cuddled up to me the whole trip down. It was quite humorous because the baby was pretty active and kicking frequently. When the dog had her head against my belly and suddenly there was movement, she'd react to that activity by quickly lifting and titling her head as she looked ever so curiously at my stomach. I could hear her say, "What was that?"

J. C. Soucier

It seemed like in no time I was at the Portland exit. Just a few more miles to go and then the mystery would be unveiled. My curiosity was really peaking. I guess that was a good sign. I was not at all concerned about getting emotionally beaten at this meeting. I was ready to face the storm head on and to deal with the inevitable. I knew that I was meeting with a man who was on a mission. I gathered that he felt the same way about me.

I was fully aware that the Church saw my baby as a threat to Matthew and to herself. This was going to be the moment when everything would need to be completed. Somebody within the inner circle of the Catholic Church had given Matthew the money with which to pay for an abortion—a direct indication that the mission was to protect at all cost. Matthew had to go back to them with the news that I had not allowed the abortion to be performed. Hence, the problem still existed. Now what? The bottom line was to get the baby out of Maine and not let me return with him. My attitude was bring on the dragon, my slingshot was loaded.

There it was, rather modest rectory, I thought. It certainly wasn't as elaborate looking as was the building Matthew lived in. Probably didn't have marble floors, two kitchens and multiple bathrooms either. I was being catty; at this point, it was my salvation, my strength-building exercise. I drove into a very short, narrow driveway positioned between two dwellings. In the dark it would be a little spooky.

As I looked at the structure, I couldn't help but think of how well-camouflaged the insurmountable amount of power was that lay beyond the walls of that brick superstructure.

"Well, here goes, girl. I'll be back shortly," I said to my dog as I hugged her. Checking to make sure that all the windows were down to give her enough air yet high enough to prevent her from jumping out. I opened the car door and stepped out. I climbed up a few stone steps to the door and rang the bell. Father DeVille immediately appeared, almost as though he'd been standing there awaiting my arrival.

"Thank you for coming, Kate," he said as he greeted me. "Please, do come in."

I followed him into the kitchen. He offered me a chair at the kitchen table. That in itself was a bit odd. I'm sure that there was an office in this rectory, or at least a room somewhat more formal and official than a kitchen. But, for whatever reason, that was the chosen spot where we were to meet. He made that very clear when he walked to the opposite side of this table and sat down.

"Kate, how can I impress upon you how grateful I am that you not only came tonight but on such short notice? I'm sure that you'll understand the urgency as we converse here. This is a very serious matter, very serious."

"Go on please, Father." I responded.

"Matthew is ill, very ill. He is having such a horrible time with this whole ordeal. Since his parents are not aware of this situation, he's limited as to where he can go to escape. They're very close you know and not being available to them increases the pressure that he is feeling."

"Oh...?" I answered tilting my head and raising my eyebrows.

Father continued.

"He's at his godmother's. He has told her about the baby. She not only understands the need for the strictest of confidence but her home has become a safe haven for him. He's free to go there whenever he needs respite. The only other person aware of this, as you know, is his sister. Kate, if ever his parents found out, they would be devastated. Matthew cannot bear the thought of his mother ever finding out that his vocation has been desecrated. He's convinced that news of this sort would kill her."

"Oh....." I said.

"Kate, you're the only person who can remedy this situation. Not only is Matthew's priesthood in the balance, his mental state faces destruction."

"Oh....."

"You see, he just can't take the combination of parishioners knowing, priests knowing, parents knowing, all compounded by the fact that this child will be growing up right under his very eyes and he won't be a part of his life."

"Oh....."

"You can remove all that pressure and help him bounce back to his old self, Kate. He is such a good priest and so loved by his parishioners. He has done so much good for so many. Sick, he just can't function."

"Oh….." I said as I thought of how much longer it would be before I would drive DeVille absolutely out of his mind with my passive aggressiveness.

"All you have to do is give up the baby, Kate. How much more simple can a solution be? I don't mean to sound insensitive because I realize that it would be a very difficult decision for you, but it would save everyone. It's the only way. Everything will be taken care of; you'll have no worries. We will handle it all."

"I'm sure you will. Let me see if I understand this correctly. The path that I am following now makes me a terrible Christian. It makes me an irresponsible Catholic, a selfish woman who will not only ruin the reputation of a fine priest and tarnish the good name of the Church, but who will knowingly rob her child of a good life. Adding salt to a wound, this decision would become a life-long sentence, a scarlet letter if you will, for the baby. Do I have that right, Father?"

"Exactly right, Kate."

"Now then, if I give up my baby, it will be Matthew's salvation. He will be relieved of all these undue pressures, the Church will go unscathed and my child will live happily ever after with a family that will give him absolutely everything this world has to offer. Is that right?"

"That's absolutely right, Kate," Father responded.

"Except his birthmother," I quickly interjected.

"But he won't miss what he never had, Kate. Don't let your mind wander unnecessarily. You seem to have come around to the right way of thinking. This is the way that will guide everybody's life back to normal. That's wonderful."

I leaned forward and in a very soft voice said, "I will burn in hell before I ever give up my baby. Your threats, Father, your accusations, your predictions do not intimidate me in the least. I am carrying my baby and I will carry him to term. I will deliver in my hometown and I will raise him in the very best way that I possibly can. And so, I'll be alone with him. I'm not afraid, we will be just fine. Father, is that clear?"

Perfect

The sling shot had been pulled and released. Target hit – bull's eye!

Father DeVille looked at me with an expression that will forever remain embedded in my mind. His frown was deep, his eyes piercing—perhaps not quite as penetrating as were mine. He never uttered a word. He rose from his chair and pointed to the door. I happily followed his unspoken directions.

As I began walking out, I stopped dead in my tracks, turned to this priest and said, "Please, tell Matthew that I still and always will love him with all my heart and that our baby is a boy."

Of course I didn't know that for a fact, but I felt secure in sharing that presumption. As I continued out the door I never turned back. I got into my car, hugged Sabrina and gently patted my tummy.

"Another dragon slain, another demon defeated. There mustn't be many more."

I looked around and felt like I had conquered the world.

We'll make it, precious little one. We're a team, a strong team, and we'll make it. Sabrina, not wanting to be left out, nuzzled her nose under my arm. She lay down beside me and slowly dropped her head to rest on my belly. I loved my life. The mountains and valleys in this journey just made me appreciate the beauty of diversity. It really was perfect.

CHAPTER 36

It was nearly the end of August, and I had another six weeks or so to go before my due date. It seemed like an eternity. I had gained weight, some forty pounds and I waddled like a duck. I found the heat extremely uncomfortable. The temperature had risen to some ungodly level, making the nights very challenging. As a result, I took frequent cat naps throughout the day. Usually I would stretch out on a lawn chair on the deck. By midday, the shaded portion of the deck would become my very own retreat. Most usually, that's where I could be found.

Once Dr. Martin felt confident that the threat of losing my baby no longer existed, my medical appointments had been spaced out a little. Now, since the time was getting closer, I was back to my weekly visits with him. I actually looked forward to my checkups, not only because the office was air conditioned, but because I was able to hear my baby's heartbeat. The doctor would put the monitor on my tummy immediately upon my arrival, and it stayed there for the duration of my visit. I so enjoyed that wonderful, melodic sound of this precious little life preparing to greet the world. Dr. Martin was very good to me. Our relationship combined trust, good chemistry and a great deal of mutual respect. He appreciated that I had sheer determination and firmness with my gentleness. He once told me that if the truth be known, the mere fact that my baby survived the physical and emotional pressures that I had experienced was nothing short of a miracle. With that in mind, he wasn't about to deprive me of any privilege that involved my baby.

Who knows how we did this, I would think. Back when I was hospitalized, the admitting diagnosis was that I was in this process of spontaneously aborting my pregnancy. There would be no

J. C. Soucier

stopping this course of action. Only God knows why that didn't happen. I wish I could take the credit for saving my baby's life, but it was God's decision. Actually, in saving my baby, He saved two lives.

It had to have been the hottest summer on record—or was it that I was so pleasantly full that every extra degree of heat felt like ten? At one point I wondered if Father Deville's prediction that I would burn in hell for my decision had a premature beginning. Although my mother and I fanned ourselves as quickly as our wrists would waver, the hot air was far too intense to diffuse.

Most often, we ate out on the deck, but on this particular evening, it seemed a little cooler indoors so, inside is where we dined. I had washed and dried the dishes from the lobster salad that we had eaten and my mother and I were sitting at the kitchen table deeply engaged in a game of Scrabble. Our competition was interrupted by the sound of footsteps on the porch. I looked up, and there stood Father Walter Wellman. Father Wellman was a dear man; he and Matthew shared the same parish. Looking less than graceful, and totally defying the law of gravity, I managed to pick myself up and toddle my way to greet our totally unexpected visitor.

"Kate, it's so good to see you," he said with a big smile on his face as he reached out to hug me.

"What a pleasant surprise, Father," was my response. "You know my mother, right?"

"I do, and how are you faring in this terrible heat?"

"I'm doing well," said my mother. "I'm losing at Scrabble tonight, though, and I blame the heat." She laughed.

"Please Father, sit down. Can I get you a cold beverage or water?" I asked.

"Water, please, Kate," Father responded.

"Mother, would you like something as well?"

She nodded yes, and softly said, "Water as well, please."

While I poured water for all of us, my mother and Father Wellman chatted. I served them both and returned to the cupboard to fill my glass. I then joined them at the table. We exchanged pleasantries. It seemed nice to chat with a priest without having to engage in a self preservation strategy. I didn't expect that it would come to an end, but it did.

"Could I speak with you privately, Kate?" Father said.

"It was nice seeing you again, Father," said my mother as she skillfully maneuvered her wheelchair and headed out of the kitchen and toward the deck.

Father Wellman went to her, placed his hand on her shoulder and simply said, "God bless you."

Father returned to his chair. Maintaining uncomfortable silence, his eyes were looking down at the Scrabble game in progress when he said in a less than assertive tone of voice, "I wish this was just a social visit, but I've come as a messenger for the Bishop, Kate."

"And so," I said, "you're here as a messenger for the bishop? Okay, you're allowed. And what would that message be, Father?"

"Kate, please remember that I am simply the messenger, and I want to apologize for that, I just have no choice."

"Uh, oh...here we go again," I thought. Is there going to be no end to this coercion? I really thought they had covered all the bases; I was wrong---what now? Father Wellman wasn't moving. He wasn't looking up, he wasn't speaking. It was as though suddenly, everything was frozen in time. After waiting a few moments with nothing happening, I made a move.

"Father, go on, please, go on," I said.

And so he did. He reached into the inside of his left breast pocket and took out a long, white envelope. It was bulging. Two brown elastics, one at each end, held it closed. He placed the wrapper on the table and gently tried to push it across to me. The bands around the envelope made a smooth transition to my side of the 1960 vintage table a bit challenging, almost an omen, as though it was hesitating in making the transfer.

I looked up at my visitor.

"What? What is this?" I asked.

He was nervous, jittery and couldn't look me straight in the eyes. He himself had been married and had children. Widowed, he was what is referred to as a late vocation because he entered the seminary late in life. Finally, he looked up at me, and dropping his head in what almost appeared to be shame, he whispered ever so softly. "There's three thousand dollars in cash in that envelope, Kate. It's your money to do with as you please. One stipulation: you must leave Maine immediately to have your baby and return alone. Your accommodations, medical expenses and adoption process will all be taken care of."

Responding to this was disheartening for me. I recognized the difficult position that Father Wellman was in; I also knew that the person whom I really wanted sitting across from me was perhaps in his office at the chancery. I had to decide how to handle this without shooting the messenger. The chances of getting to the root of it all were perhaps minimal, and I wasn't certain that I even wanted to bother to take it to that extreme. Should I extend this saga by handling the return message myself? Or was there a way of getting the job done effectively without compromising Father Wellman's role in all of this? Because after all, he was only fulfilling his vow of obedience to his bishop.

"I'm sorry that you were chosen to deliver this message, Father. It must have been the luck of the draw. I truly believe that you're feeling compromised about being in this position. I wish I could spare you the anguish of further involvement in this difficult situation. But I guess there's no way of changing the players on this field. So, I need to respond. And, I need to reply to the bishop's, what shall I call it... buyoff? Bribe? Enticement? Incentive? Corrupting gift? Present? Or would it be just plain envelope? Can you deliver it verbatim, Father?"

"Verbatim is verbatim, Kate," he responded. "If I give you my word that I will deliver your message word for word, then that's exactly what I will do. It's what the bishop would expect of me, I'm sure."

"Okay, since you will be directly quoting my words, you will then not be held responsible for how I express my reply. Correct?

"That's right, Kate," Father answered.

"That's perfect. I'm not sure that once you hear what I have to say you'll be anxious to go back to your bishop with my response, but then, verbatim is verbatim and that is my wish."

"I'm listening, Kate?'

Perfect

I apologized sincerely for what was to follow. Then, I took Father Wellman's hand, placed the envelope in his palm, forcing him to clench his fist. I stared him squarely in the eyes and clearly enunciated my message to the bishop. Without another word, I walked out of the room, leaving Father to show himself out.

Was the mission ever completed? Yes…I'm certain that Father returned the envelope to the bishop accompanied by a message. However, was the message verbatim? Whether or not my exact words ever reached the bishop's ears will always remain unknown and perhaps it is just as well. One thing is certain, another dragon was slain.

CHAPTER 37

A lthough several days had passed, I couldn't get out of my mind the energy and resources that the Church had put into making the disappearance of my baby happen. Absolutely no one heard my words or wishes. Neither my baby nor I seemed to matter at all. It was all about Matthew. That had made me angry and strong. I wasn't angry at God, nor was I angry at the Church. The words that Reverend Matthew McGee once uttered as he delivered the sermon titled "The Catholic Crisis" summed up my feelings perfectly:

"I am outraged not at the Catholic Church but at those within the Catholic Church who have perpetuated and protected such destructive behavior."

I had certainly experienced an interesting pregnancy, eventful indeed. The bickering and upheavals had almost become a game. I was no longer vulnerable to the threats and intimidations, the verbal rape, the attempts at disarming a human being until nothing is left but a submissive second-class citizen. No more—that was in direct violation of my space and my person and would happen no more. Every one of these experiences had been initiated by someone connected to the Roman Catholic Church. The abortion arrangements were not made by a Catholic clergy, but Matthew had initiated it and someone within the Church provided Matthew with the money for the trip, elaborate hotel accommodations, gourmet dinner, beautiful roses and the abortion that although never happened, was scheduled and therefore paid for.

It seemed as though I was attacked from a different flank almost every month. In March, it was the trip to New York for the abortion followed by my hospitalization and Matthew's visit. A merciful break came in April. Then came the driving suggestion from

J. C. Soucier

Eloise to have an abortion. In May, great news for some - Matthew was transferred to a parish 20 miles away and elevated to pastor. Whether that was a reward for his behavior, decision to stay within the church or incentive to get well soon will remain a mystery - interesting though.

The heat of summer was punctuated by multiple discussions with Church clergy. June and July included trips to meet Father DeVille. Under pressure from the Bishop, Father Wellman visited with another adoption plea.

And now September... I was somewhat curious as to what awaited me in the wings this month.

Amazing to have had all this activity, all these people engaged in saving the reputation of a priest—not the life of a child—but the reputation of a priest! The puzzle remained unsolved in my mind. I just couldn't understand how the miracle of birth, the sacredness of life being God's greatest gift, could be so disrespected by the very men who professed its sanctity.

I walked out onto the deck to join my mother.

"How did it go, Kate? Did you have a pleasant visit with Father Wellman?"

"Not really, mother—he didn't come on a social visit. He was here as a messenger of the bishop."

"I see," she said.

"The bishop offered me three thousand dollars to have my baby adopted."

"*Maudit argent*," she said in French. Damn money. This was another display of behavior very out of character for my mother. I was nearly twenty-nine years old and had never heard her even come close to using a disrespectful word. Her reaction was just what the doctor ordered. That diffused my frustrations completely and allowed me to forget the thoughts that were rambling through my mind. I relaxed.

Iced tea was the thirst quencher before bed; it hit the spot. I slid into my bed, cuddled my very, very rotund belly, smiled and whispered, it's just you and me, Babe.

Then it happened. From a sound sleep, I awoke and looked at the clock on the table at my bedside. It read nine minutes past ten.

168

Perfect

"Christian," I said out loud. "Christian! That will be his name." I turned on the light, took paper and pen from the nightstand and wrote the letters: C H R I S T I A N. And so, at 10:09 that evening, I had my very first and eternal gift for my son—his name.

CHAPTER 38

T he day when I would finally meet this very important little person was now within striking distance. I had been saintly patient, and now, it was time. Hopefully, this eventful day would be celebrated on schedule. My suitcase was packed and ready to go. It contained my personal items; birth announcements that I had made heralding the birth of my son, his coming-home outfit and the bunting and blanket that his grandmother had bought for the occasion. I didn't think twice about how ill-equipped I was if I were to deliver a daughter. I wasn't concerned in the least because I knew deep down in my heart that I would bring a son into this world. I trusted my natural instinct and believed.

The waiting game had begun. It was said over and over again that most women in their final days of pregnancy want to deliver and just get it over with. Odd as it may be, I didn't feel that way. Perhaps because I had been through so much to keep this pregnancy I wasn't about to complain. I had worked hard to gain the right to carry this baby and having done that, I didn't want the process to be short-circuited in any way. I wanted my nine months—and I got them.

I waited patiently. I had learned to knit, not well, but I did make a blanket whose rows intertwined to lock together and ultimately was wonderful in keeping the blanket securely wrapped around the baby. That became my favorite. In addition to knitting, I spent a great deal of time reading a variety of children's stories and singing to Christian. The song that I serenaded him with over and over again was *"Music, Laughter and Tears,"* written and sung by Deanna Edwards. The song tells of important gifts that a mother can give her child; gifts that would "never grow old," those being music, laughter and tears.

I sang this song to him frequently during the day and every single night. This soothing and very beautiful song was slowly earning the privilege of becoming the traditional bedtime lullaby in our home. I rocked I rubbed my belly and softly sang those lyrics. Christian approved. He loved it and reacted to it. He'd give me his few little kicks of approval and then his level of activity in utero seemed to quiet down as he contently settled in for a nap.

On one particular morning I awoke hardly able to face the day, I was so excited. Finally, it was time! October 5 was here— my due date! I so wanted to believe that because it was my due date, Christian would automatically follow suit and make his entrance into this world. Well, my due date was not Christian's choice. October 5 came, October 5 went and…no change. I was still pregnant.

I had resigned myself to the fact that I was not controlling this show, Christian was. He would make his debut when he was good and ready; meanwhile, I would continue to wait.

It was mid-morning on Saturday, October 7. A friend and I had walked to my Aunt Julia's to visit with her and have a cup of tea. As we were walking back home, uncontrollable streams of warm water ran down my legs. This could really be one of two things, I thought. As it ended what could have been a simple loss of bladder control and a bit embarrassing turned into a very joyful moment. My water had broken! "This is it!" I called out to the world. "This is it! It's time—finally it's time." I was sparkling with energy.

"Okay, let's get home quickly and I'll call the doctor. Meanwhile, you can put my suitcase in my car, ok?"

"Any contractions?" asked my friend Linda.

"No, not yet," I answered.

"Then let's just get you home, Kate. You can check with your doctor and go it from there. Chances are that baby will take his time so no need to rush." Linda had two children so childbirth wasn't totally new to her.

Somewhat uncomfortable but so looking forward to the event ahead, I may have sprinted as I rounded the corner hurrying to get home. I was moving at such a pace that Linda, totally not pregnant, lagged behind!

"Mother, this is it! My water just broke." I was exuberant, bursting at the seams, so excited! I wanted to call the doctor first, so I headed for the telephone. I dialed Dr. Martin's number that I had long ago memorized and waited for someone to answer. I hadn't thought that this was Saturday and the answering service would pick up. Although I'd been kept abreast of his weekends off, I had not ever wanted to think that someone other than Dr. Martin could be the doc who would deliver Christian.

"Hello, Dr. Martin's answering service."

"Hello, this is Kate," forgetting that the answering service was picking up and had no clue who I was. I was so accustomed to having his office recognize my voice that I just continued to rattle on. "My water broke just minutes ago, but I haven't had any labor pains yet. What shall I do?"

"Ma'am, I just need to ask you a few questions first, including your full name."

"Oh, yes, sure."

"Wow, just a little spacey here, need to keep it together and answer correctly," I thought to myself as I proceeded to respond to the questions. Then I was told that Dr. Donahue was covering for Dr. Martin and he would be calling me back within moments.

I was devastated. I slowly put the telephone receiver back on the base and walked into the kitchen. Before I had a chance to sit, the telephone rang.

"Kate," the male voice on the other end of the phone asked.

"Yes," I replied.

"This is Dr. Donahue. I'm covering for Dr. Martin. Your water broke—are you having any contractions?"

"No, no pain yet."

"Then tell me exactly what's happened, please."

"I was walking home from having had tea with my aunt and my water broke. No pain, just lots and lots of water."

"That's normal. Now, you need to come to the hospital. No big hurry. Just relax, gather your things and come up to maternity. The nurses will make you very comfortable, and I'll be there shortly. I'll check you and we'll see what's going on. Tell me, are you feeling any pressure on your cervix?"

"Not really, not more than usual," I answered.

"And no urge to push…"

"No, Doctor Donahue, nothing at all."

"Okay then," he said, "Come along at your own pace."

I was a little bit anxious about going to the hospital, not because I was frightened but because I was leaving the very secure environment of my home and going to a hospital setting to have my baby. I had mixed emotions. I was so looking forward to delivering my son, but…with Dr. Martin guiding me through; now, that was all changed. With no idea what to expect, it was first things first, so, I took a shower—a fast shower.

Before leaving, I took one last look around to make certain that everything was ready and perfect for when Christian would come home. I had placed his cradle next to my bed. All the linen had been washed as well as all his baby clothes. His little outfits had been hung in a baby armoire and little undershirts were folded neatly in the drawers. The room actually smelled "baby clean." The musical mobile had been placed above his cradle; the cassette tape deck had been moved into the bedroom and was ready to go with classical tapes to play while he slept. Diapers, bottles and baby books were ready. The bases had been covered.

Ready to head out, I was trying to convince my friend Linda that I could easily drive myself to the hospital. As I bent over to hug my mother, she said in her soft voice, "I am so happy for you, Kate. You've worked hard and waited long for this day. You have earned every moment of happiness that my grandson will bring you. I don't like the idea of you driving yourself to the hospital though. Linda's right here; why not let her go with you, settle you in and then she can bring your car back?" Willing to compromise in order to comfort my mother's anxieties, I agreed.

"I will be just fine, and you're right, Mother, I have worked hard and have no regrets. I feel sorry for Matthew though—he will never share the joys that this baby will bring. Oh well." I walked toward the door, knelt down, hugged and petted Sabrina. I turned to wave to my mother.

"Good luck, dear. Call me as soon as that baby is born, promise?"

"Promise. Just think, Mom, this is the very last time that I walk through this door alone. The next time, not only will I be a mother, but I'll be holding your brand new grandson."

"You're so convinced that you are going to deliver a boy, Kate, I hope you're not disappointed."

"Worry not, I won't be." I smiled, blew the world a kiss and proudly strutted out to my car, Linda in tow. Just a few more minutes I thought, and then...

CHAPTER 39

I drove to the hospital and parked in the short-term parking lot. Linda and I entered and went directly up to maternity. The nurse had been notified of my arrival. She led me to my room, handed me a hospital Johnny and was extremely pleasant.

"This is your first baby?"

"Yes it is. I sure am anxious to be holding him in my arms!" I said bubbling with excitement. "I can hardly wait!"

"Some of these little ones take their time. They're probably so comfortable in their mom that the journey out isn't too inviting. At least you know that the longest part of your wait is over. It's but a matter of hours now…"

"Yes…few hours, I hope!"

"Dr. Donahue will be here shortly."

I changed, hung items in the small closet that was provided, and placed magazines, a deck of cards and my knitting on the side table. I looked down the hallway for Linda and saw her waiting by the nurse's station. She pointed to a tall man who was talking with one of the nurses and she silently spoke the word doctor. I retreated back into my room and continued investigating what would be my living quarters for the next few days. Within moments, there was a light knock on my door.

"May I come in?" the strange voice uttered.

"Certainly," I responded.

"I'm Dr. Donahue, Kate. I'll be taking over for Dr. Martin because it's his weekend off. He's back on at 8 a.m. on Monday. By then, the work will be over and you'll have your baby to show him."

"Oh, I see," I said, trying to hide the disappointment in my voice.

J. C. Soucier

I'm quite certain that the good doctor realized that I was disappointed with the alteration to the plan; I had such a good rapport with Dr. Martin. "Oh well," I thought, "not a whole lot I can do about this so might just as well go with the flow."

Dr. Donahue seemed sensitive to my feelings. He asked me to lie on my bed and he put me through the usual routine to check out what was happening as I entered the beginning stage of the delivery process.

"We need to admit you, Kate, although I don't expect that little guy of yours to hurry out. Since your water broke, I don't want to chance any infection. Please settle in and your nurse will bring in the paperwork. The drawback to this hotel is that the kitchen is closed until after the baby is born—except for popsicles and ice chips. You can have as many of those as you want. Sorry," he said gently as he placed his hand on my shoulder and squeezed it gently. He went on to say, "I won't be far away."

Within a few minutes, my nurse entered my room.

"Hi! My name is Claire. We'll be joined at the hip until you're discharged, Kate, so I'd best learn what kind of popsicles you like early in the game. While you complete this paperwork, I'll go get your first one. Choice of flavor, ma'am?"

"I really like raspberry, at least for starters."

"Raspberry it will be. I'll stock up on that flavor so we don't run out. Meanwhile, your first one is coming right up!"

Linda had been in, made of list of what she thought I might need and left assuring me that she'd return later in the day. Meanwhile, I filled out the forms and had completed them by the time my raspberry popsicle was delivered. My throat was dry and that icy cold sweet taste certainly quenched my thirst. "Feel free to walk around the floor, Kate. Exercise can only help activate that labor."

That was all I needed to hear. I paced up and down that floor for what seemed to be hours. Did it jump start my labor? No.

It was 3:35 p.m. on October 7, 1972. I had walked around the unit many times over, had met all the nurses at shift change and had gone through three glasses of ice chips, and I'd only been there for a little more than three hours.

Perfect

Linda returned accompanied by a couple of friends. We ended up in the waiting room because although at the time I was the only expectant mom on the floor, five new moms were patients and babies were out in their rooms. The newborn count was three girls and two boys. I was going to even that out.

About ten o'clock that evening a woman was admitted in full labor. She arrived and never made it to the room. Within one hour of her admittance, she birthed her daughter and was in the recovery room. How I envied her!

I went in and chatted with the new mom. Her beautiful, healthy daughter weighed in at ten pounds, twelve ounces—quite a package to deliver. I returned to my room and turned on television. After watching for a little bit, I curled up and cuddled my round belly as I did every night before falling asleep. The time was very close now. As I closed my eyes, I heard myself talking to Christian.

Okay, whenever you're ready, Babe, it will not be too soon. I'm so anxious to actually hold you in my arms; it can't be much longer now, right? I do hope that you like your name. I can't take credit for giving you such a beautiful, powerful, meaningful name. I'm not even sure where it comes from. Perhaps it's a title, an honored title that before you were even born, you earned. I don't know, Christian, for whatever reason it just fits. Goodnight, sweet baby, maybe tomorrow…or, even anytime tonight…it would be fine if you woke me to make your grand entrance into this world.

CHAPTER 40

Tomorrow came and tomorrow went. October 8 was totally uneventful. Fortunately several of my friends visited and we had a couple of hours of challenging poker. I didn't win at any of those games either. As for the evening, it was quiet. My mother surprised me and came to visit with Aunt Julia and Jeanne. After they left, I chatted with the nurses for a while and discovered that they too were longing for activity from my little guy. In spite of the multiple cheerleaders who were waiting to herald this birth, this tiny little person was controlling it all. Another day came...and it just didn't happen.

I was awake at the crack of dawn on Monday, October 9. This had to be the day; popsicles and ice chips were getting pretty old and I was getting very hungry. I did have a bit of an odd feeling—not bad, not good—just odd. The sunrise was so pretty; it had that burnt orange gold tint to it, giving the morning a warm glow. Snow had been predicted but there was no sign of precipitation in the sky. "This would be a perfect day," I thought, "but how do I get that message across to my baby?"

My daydreaming was interrupted as I heard this gentle voice say, "You waited all weekend for me." It was Dr. Martin. There he was in the doorway of my room smiling from ear to ear.

"I did; now work your magic and let's get this show on the road, Dr. Martin!"

It was shortly before eight o'clock and Dr. Martin was back to work. Apparently, that was Christian's clue. Within minutes after Dr. Martin's arrival, I felt my first labor pain. How coincidental was that? Or was it? Was my son sensitive to my needs even before we were formally introduced and he'd waited to feel that tender touch and hear his kind voice? After all, it all began when

J. C. Soucier

Dr. Martin was slowly walking his hands over my abdomen to gage the baby's position, so he felt it too. It wasn't my imagination; it was a real labor pain. How I had waited for this! Another came and then another. The nurse was calculating the time from one contraction to another. I was averaging about six minutes between pains. Although it would probably still be a while, at least the actual process had begun!

"Okay, Kate. The baby has decided to make his move. You'll probably be working most of the day. I'm guessing that late afternoon, early evening and that baby will be in your arms. How about we have a dinner date in your room after you deliver that son of yours?"

"Yes! Absolutely, how about we eat at my place?" I said with a smirk on my face.

"Your place it is," he responded. "That sense of humor will see you through a whole lot, Kate, don't ever lose it!"

"Okay, Doc. See you soon!"

Had I said soon? Well, it wasn't quite that soon. I spent a long, labor intensive day; but I knew every step of the way that with every hour, every pain, I was that much closer to meeting my son. It all happened at 4:01 p.m.

"Congratulations, Kate. Finally, you have a beautiful, healthy son—and you'd better believe that his waterworks...work very well!"

At last I was holding my long-awaited, newly born son in my arms.

"Give her the time she needs, please, no hurry to move out of here," were Dr. Martin's gentle orders. They followed them. He knew only too well what I had gone through to get to this moment; he wasn't going to allow anyone to rob me of this beginning.

"My very first gift to you will be the most important, my son; and that is your name. Christian, beautiful, so very sweet Christian." I held his firm seven pounds, thirteen ounce body close to mine. I just couldn't get enough of him.

The nurses were very kind. Instead of taking him directly to the nursery, they allowed him to remain on me while they rolled me out of delivery. We made a stop at the nursery door where they took him to clean him up and run the usual routine tests for newborns. Before leaving him, I asked Dr. Martin if I could give him his first feeding of water and sugar that usually the nursery nurses would handle.

"Of course, Kate, he's your son; you have every right to feed him. The first feeding needs to be done in the nursery for them to monitor his ability to suck and swallow. They'll wake you when the time comes."

"Thank you. Please don't forget, will you?" The nurse who was walking away with Christian smiled at me and nodded.

"Bet you're a little hungry, Mom; how about we have that dinner now?" Dr. Martin blurted out.

"Great, Doc—my place, right?"

He laughed. The nurses wheeled me into recovery and put me in a nice clean bed with an abundant number of pillows. Not much later I heard Dr. Martin's voice as he rounded the corner into my room. He was pushing a cart crowded with over-sized plates that held a steak, carrots, green beans and a baked potato. Included was a huge glass of diet Pepsi loaded with ice for me and a cup of coffee for himself.

"Yummy," I said with vigor. "You cannot imagine how wonderful that looks to me. Next to my son, right this very minute, this meal is second in standings!" I said in a voice that one would expect hearing from a child at Christmas. I ate every single morsel. Dr. Martin left nothing behind either.

I took a quick minute to call my mother. She was so excited.

"I'll be there to visit tonight, Kate. Can I bring you anything?" she asked.

"I'm all set, Mom. Wait until you meet your grandson. He's perfect! See you in a little bit."

Doc Martin had lifted his cup of coffee, I my glass of soda and we carefully hit them together as he toasted.

"This is in celebration of one hell of a pregnancy, Kate. Good work, no, great work!" I was proud; I was so very proud.

The meal was delicious and the company so delightful. Once we had finished, I was ready to sneak in a quick nap before com-

J. C. Soucier

pany arrived. But first I walked to the nursery to visit my son. As I returned to my room, a figure in a black suit was looking out the window. I walked in, said hello in a questioning tone of voice, and the figure turned toward me.

"Congratulations on the birth of your son," said Father Wellman.

"Thank you. Word travels mighty fast, doesn't it? Were you just in the neighborhood, Father?" I asked.

"No, Kate. We do have our ways of knowing certain things. I would love to meet your son. Shall we go to the nursery together?"

"Certainly Father, it will be my pleasure." I couldn't help but think of the last time that he and I had met; our encounter was not quite as pleasant back then as it would be today. I thought about asking him whether or not my message had ever reached the bishop. I chose to drop it because I really didn't want to tarnish the memories of October 9, 1972.

We walked down the hall to the nursery. Christian was sleeping comfortably, wrapped in a blue blanket. The little name card inserted in the holder at the head of the crib identified which baby was mine.

Instantly, Father's reaction was, "My, he certainly looks like his father, don't you think?"

"It's in the eyes of the beholder, Father. He's healthy and he's beautiful and he's here, with me! That's what really matters."

"Matthew is at his godmother's and has been deathly ill all day. Just can't seem to stop vomiting. He called me and asked that I come to make certain that you and the baby were fine."

"How sweet that is of him. Do share the good news."

He dropped his head as we turned to return to my room.

"Yes, Kate, you did the right thing. I saw the depth of love that fed your strength. Good for you---and for Christian! I'll tell Matthew, Kate; and, I so hope that all goes well for you both. God bless you and Christian."

"Thank you, and my best to Matthew. I do hope that he recovers from his ailment quickly. And Father, when you run into Father DeVille or the bishop, please extend to them both my warmest regards." His eyes dropped to the floor as a hint of a smile appeared on his face. He got the message; he just couldn't let me know that he understood and perhaps agreed with my sarcasm.

He left. I fell asleep. I awoke to my mother gently rubbing her hand up and down my arm. I arose quickly and within seconds my mother, aunt, cousin and I were at the nursery to see my newborn son.

It was love at first sight for my mother. I could see the sparkle in her eyes, the tears running down her cheeks and the joy that she radiated.

"I'm a grandmother," she said very, very softly, "thank you."

CHAPTER 41

I was sitting comfortably in a rocking chair in a private room off the nursery with Christian cuddled safely in my arms. As I gave him his first feeding, his bright blue eyes stared at his proud mother and his little mouth was ever so busy suckling the sugar and water combination. I looked at my newborn son and smiled. As I glanced out the window, the bright moon showcased beautifully as it lit the sky. Huge snowflakes gracefully floated down from the heavens landing ever so gently on the wide windowsills. Amazing! October 9 and there was snow—a little early, even for Maine. I put down the bottle, stood up and held Christian upright against my chest, hoping that maybe, just maybe, he would be seeing his first snowflakes on the day of his birth. Although it is said that newborns see primarily shadows, who really knows that? What new baby has given us that information? Just in the case that these brand new little people have more sophisticated eyesight than we realized I wanted Christian to have the opportunity, from the very beginning, to see the beauty that awaited him as he would journey through life.

"This is such a unique greeting for you, Christian, a salutation in honor of your birth. Your birthday will always be a very special day because it will celebrate the beginning of a very exceptional, distinctive life."

It was at this time that I made a vow to my newborn son. I promised that I would be with him as long as God was willing and would do everything in my power to give him all the opportunities to become the man that I knew he was capable of being.

"You, my son, will become the best of the best, a global citizen, wonderful, loyal husband, dedicated dad, committed family man, a professional with integrity, loyal friend, devoted son, loving son-in-law, and much, much more. I promise you my life as an enrichment to help make this world a far better place for you, your family and all who will follow. For now, it's just you and me, Babe, and together, we'll make it. When the day comes that this combination changes, I will forever be in the background as a support to the new team that will take the lead."

After the feeding and a diaper change, I brought Christian to my room. I placed him on my bed as he napped. I sat by his side just watching him sleep, gently stroking his delicate, angelic face with the side of my thumb. My thoughts wandered to Matthew.

The relationship that I shared with Christian's father would forever be cherished. We had such special times; the moonlit walks, the dancing fires, the boat trips, the hearty laughter, Johnny Carson, walking hand in hand in the rain, dancing through freshly made puddles, making s'mores over open fires on the rocks, cuddling, and yes...the bear-skin rug always to be remembered as the bed of sweet surrender. It was deep, pure, committed love; perhaps far too intense to survive.

With this profound feeling for another person, there comes the vulnerability and willingness to plummet the distance. And I did. Therefore, to focus only on the good times would be very dangerous, the need to recognize the not so good times...real. The periods within our relationship that were painful were agonizingly so. There were days when the hurt was so excruciating that I really didn't think that I had what was needed to go on. I was lonely...so lonely with no one to comfort me, no one to guide me, no one to renew my strength. My pregnancy, my son, became my focal point that saved my life.

Observing Matthew's actions finally gave me the strength to sever our relationship. On that fateful day while I was in the hospital struggling with every ounce of strength to keep my pregnancy, and Matthew came to visit, it was then that I was able to see through the shadows of his many colors. I didn't blame him and I will always love him. There was no room in his life for us, and on that day I was able to accept the truth and move on.

All the memories would be forever treasured, because these tell our history, the times past and how it all began. As deep, pure and committed as our love was, let it never be forgotten that it was forbidden. That's why all those precious moments that we had together were so perfect. They had to be. We both knew that our love would live forever, but as much as I wanted to believe that someday we would unite our lives, I just knew from the very bottom of my heart that we would not have that privilege. Because of this, every instant together had to be flawless, absolute, a masterpiece. I would always believe that I was born to love this very man and to give birth to our son. Over the course of my life that love would rise to a much higher level. It would reach a plane that was totally beyond describing. That's just the way it would always be.

With my eyes gazing at Christian, I couldn't resist any longer. "Sweet, sweet baby…you're just the most beautiful little cherub." I gently slid my hands under his perfect little body and carefully lifted him from the softness of the bed. Sitting upright, I gingerly leaned into the fluffy pillows. I cradled the love of my life in my arms. Staring at his radiant little face, I whispered:

"You know, my angelic baby, everything about you is quite unique. As I think of how your name was chosen, that's pretty intriguing. I awoke one night out of a deep sleep for no apparent reason. The name C-H-R-I-S-T-I-A-N was bouncing relentlessly in my head. That's it! No second thought, no deliberations—the decision had been made.

"Christian will become my son's name," I remember saying loudly. I remember noting the time on my alarm clock as I reached for pen and paper; it had read 10:09 p.m.

"10-09, Christian," I continued to say, "how coincidental is that? 10-09 was not only the time when I awoke with your name in my mind but it is also today's date – your birth date!"

As I continued to stroke Christian's glowing face he smiled, most likely from the tickling sensation that he was feeling, but the timing was good. I loved it. In total ecstasy, I drifted into the future envisioning that this tiny, perfect little being asleep in my arms would someday be the reflection to generations to come, of a love between two people that although too perfect to survive, will live forever. As tears filled my eyes, I kissed Christian's forehead.

J. C. Soucier

"Matthew, it's been a wild and wonderful ride. Thank you for being my perfect man, for sharing the experience of a perfect love and for giving me the perfect gift."

EPILOGUE

Nearly forty years have gone by and...

My mother has passed away.

Lois and I still remain very good friends and in constant communication.

Doctor Martin has retired and his oldest son has taken over his practice.

Father Deville has died. However, he received several promotions between our meetings and his death. He became a Monsignor and ultimately, in 1975, was named to the Episcopacy for the Diocese and was consecrated Auxiliary Bishop.

Matthew never left the priesthood. He met his son, spent limited time with him, but passed on the opportunity to discover what a treasure he had co-created. Now, in his early seventies, he is experiencing a great deal of memory loss and is unable to live independently. He is a resident in a local nursing home facility. Occasionally, Jeanne and I have taken Matthew to an out of town restaurant for lunch. The last time we were together his icy blue eyes that were once so bright and sparkling were baron of any life and the lack of his entertaining humor was blatantly obvious. It was clear that his memory loss was more severe and his recognizance ability perhaps totally gone. He has, although undergoing all these changes, managed to retain his infectious smile and joie de vivre. I think of him often and as my mind wanders to his life today, I wonder if Matthew's loss of memory is a handicap or a gift –.

Christian, now thirty-five years old, is very accomplished, and I am so very proud of him. He has found his best friend, soul mate and true love, Stephanie whom he married (and now, I have two perfect gifts). He has earned his bachelor's degree, two master degrees and his Ph.D. in biology. As a marine biologist, he is em-

J. C. Soucier

ployed as a Senior Scientist/Project Manager for a large, international environmental consulting company. The sea remains his passion. In their spare time, Christian and Stephanie are happy travelers and dabble in real estate.

As for me, I continue to love being a mother which will always be my primary focus. I have been a teacher, social worker and have recently retired following a twenty-one year tenure working for a non-profit organization. I have chosen a celibate life because I truly believe that in a totally different dimension I have to this day and forever, found my perfect love. As for my son, I willingly vowed to dedicate my total person to his wellbeing. And I have, and will continue to, until I can no more.

My life was further enriched five years ago when I found my birth family. I have a sister (whom I feel I have known forever). For sixty years I thought that I was an only child and so did she. What a grand surprise it was to find out differently! Added to that is a brother-in-law, niece, nephew, grand niece, great-grand nieces, great-grand nephew, uncle and cousins. All new! And so, the circle of family continues to grow. As I saunter into the autumn of my life, I do so with the accompaniment of my three wonderful families by my side – my adoptive family, birth family and Christian's in–laws.

If I were asked: What would you change about this period of your life? In a flash and without a second thought, my response would be:

For me, I cannot imagine life without Christian. I would not change a thing. For another however, I would pass along and encourage one to heed (although I didn't) to the words of wisdom that my father once gave to me:

"Be sure that when you give your heart away, you give it to someone who is free to accept it."

Printed in the United States
210885BV00001B/148/P

9 781432 728892